AN ORMAN'S FATE

Part of the Truson S.E.T. Series

Dominique Gibson

Cover art created by Canva.

 This is a work of fiction. Any resemblance to any person, living or dead, is purely coincidental.

ISBN-13: 978-1-7329574-4-2 (Ebook)
ISBN-13: 978-1-7329574-5-9 (Hardcover)
ISBN-13: 978-1-73295746-6 (Paperback)

Dedication

I would like to dedicate this book to my boyfriend, Mr. Hunter, to my wonderful editor, Judy Roth, and to my family who has continued to support me on this journey. Your efforts are greatly appreciated.

Books by **Dominique Gibson**:

Paranormal Romance: **TRUSON S.E.T. SERIES:**

AN ORMAN'S REVENGE
AN ORMAN'S FATE
AN ORMAN'S ALLEGIANCE (Coming Soon)

SIGN UP FOR MY NEWSLETTER!

Do you want to keep up with the latest updates, articles, and more? Sign up for my monthly newsletter on my website at www.dominiquegibsonauthor.com or you can catch me on Facebook and Twitter to learn more. Hope to see you again real soon.

List of terms for the Truson S.E.T. Series:

The Island of Truson: An island that's located from the rest of the world that was created by Benjamin Truson and Courtney Madison for a safe hiding place for the Ormans and other species to live on after the U.S. Government declared it was no longer safe to keep them scattered throughout the world.

Ormans: A race of half-human, half-orcas that lives on the island of Truson.

Alter Ego: The animal side of the human species that rises to the surface. After being injected with the Animan three-hundred, the Ormans transform into an orca for twelve hours a day before turning back into their human form for another twelve hours. The only exception to this rule would be if the human was injected a few hours after their death as a human.

Truson Super Elite Team: A bunch of half-human, half-animal hybrids who are sworn to protect humans from criminals both on land and water.

Book of Truson: A manual that contains specific information about how the Truson S.E.T. was born, starting from ancient Egypt until the present day in addition to the laws of Truson to keep the Truson S.E.T.'s powers from spinning out of control.

The Transforments: A group of orcas that was created by Samuel Holifield as a way to retaliate revenge on the Truson S.E.T. after being kicked out of the group for killing innocent humans and Ormans throughout the years.

Binosil: A liquid medicine used to stop the human-animal transformation whenever it is too dangerous for a human to transform into their animal form.

The Hammerhead Squad: A group of half-human, half-hammerheads who have a very corrupt background when it comes to lying and murdering people.

CHAPTER ONE

*I'm sorry, Tonia. I just want to be friend*s.

Those words echoed in Tonia Ojai's mind as she downed the last sip of tequila. After all this time, she still couldn't understand why Ford just wanted to be friends with her. How could he possibly want to be friends after everything they had been through together? Tonia thought about how much of an outcast she'd been when she first turned into an Orman.

"Another shot of tequila?"

Tonia focused her attention on the bartender and smiled while handing her the glass.

"Keep it coming," she said.

"No problem." The bartender gently took the glass and walked away while Tonia stared out at the water rushing along the shores. The sun was beautiful at night and everything seemed to be cheery.

Except for your love life, of course.

"Here you go."

Tonia smiled and thanked the bartender for her service. She drank the glass of tequila and let the warm sensation flow through her throat.

"I would slow down if I were you. Our alter egos don't like it when we're drunk."

Anger boiled inside her. The sound of his voice made every feeling in her body come alive and not in a good way. She could feel her alter ego wanting to snap his neck just for disturbing her evening.

"Do you mind? I'm trying to enjoy a nice, relaxing night without anyone stalking me or telling me what to do, and I would appreciate it if you would go away and let me have the peace I deserve."

Instead of walking away, he decided to scoot next to her.

"The peace you deserve? What could have possibly happened…"

Tonia glared at him.

"Stin Vanderson, I'm only going to warn you once to stay the hell away from me."

He cocked his head to the side.

"For what it's worth, I'm sorry about what happened between you and Ford. I know how much you wanted a relationship with him," he said.

Tonia squinted.

"Great, so now you're making fun of me too?" *Don't need this right now.* Tonia got up from the counter and headed out the door, but Stin grabbed her arm.

"It wasn't a joke, Tonia. I meant every word of it. Can't imagine how you felt when Ford told you that in front of all the members of the Truson S.E.T. It must have been really embarrassing for you."

"Save your pity for someone who gives a damn." Tonia jerked her hand away but made the mistake of staring into Stin's baby blue eyes. For a second, she thought she saw something. It was a sense of anger and sadness mixed together, two emotions Tonia never knew existed when it came to Stin. *The man is capable of feelings Tonia. He is part human after all.*

"Fine," Stin said, breaking the silence. "I just wanted to show some sympathy for your situation, but if you want to continue to be a bitch for the rest of the night, then I can excuse myself and find another place to sit."

Tonia shrugged.

"By all means." It wasn't fair that he came in to spoil her night. She didn't need him to rub it in her face or give out any phony apologies.

"You know, you're not the only one having issues. I'm having a lot of problems as well, and it's way more than getting dumped by a guy," Stin said.

Tonia sighed. Why did men have to act like babies whenever something didn't go as planned?

You got room to talk sister. Look at where you are.

Tonia felt like she had no choice but to sit down and listen. Though she would have preferred to be alone, something told her Stin wasn't going to let that happen. Her eyes never left his face as she darted back into the chair.

"Since you've decided your situation is so much worse than mine, feel free to speak," she said. After the way Stin had treated her, it should have been her choice to walk away and not even give him a chance to explain himself. She remembered the horrible way he treated her in front of a bunch of students at the Truson School for Shapeshifters when she wanted to protect Ford from another group of orcas called the Transforments. They once had an argument that was so bad, Tonia almost killed him by throwing her power of acid in his face. She'd immediately apologized even though she felt like he deserved it.

"Dr. Madison is dead. My best friend is no longer single, and I'm now dealing with a sixteen-year-old boy who wanted nothing more than to prove a point to his father that he was important to him."

Tonia swallowed. Memories of Dr. Madison's torched body burned her. She didn't want to remember what happened that day, so she decided to focus on Stin.

Unfortunately for her, that stemmed a problem as well. He had the most gorgeous baby blue eyes she'd ever seen. The intensity of his eyes felt like he was staring into her soul. Her body and alter ego stirred. She convinced herself it was sadness and fear invading those eyes, and all she could do was sit and listen to whatever came next.

I guess this is how he got women to sleep with him, huh?

"What? No comment? No telling me to go to hell?" he asked. Tonia could tell he was half-joking about the comment. She shifted her weight.

"No," she finally answered. "I thought maybe you were on some BS tonight, but I can see you're in need of…" Tonia paused. "…Company."

He lifted a brow.

"Really?" He shifted closer to her. "And how can you tell I'm in need of company?"

Her mouth watered. Her arms felt like they were on fire. What the hell was happening to her? She hated this man's guts. His attitude about her made her feel breathless. *Quick! Say something to make him stop.*

"I don't know. With all the women you sleep with, I'm surprised to find you here alone. I thought you would be spending more time being in someone else's bed than sitting down at a bar having a drink," she replied.

Stin shifted back.

That worked.

"I should have known you didn't care about Dr. Madison. You don't care about anyone except yourself. I don't even see why I bothered to sit here next to you." The desire she once felt was replaced by anger.

"How dare you say I didn't care about her? I loved her more than I loved anyone else in my life." Tonia squinted. "She was the first person who helped me get out of the hell I experienced in Africa. I wanted to escape after my parents died, but I couldn't." She paused.

Stin's jaw stiffened. He turned away from her and slammed his hand down on the counter. The gesture stunned Tonia. She was expecting some sort of rude backlash or offensive comment. There was just silence.

"Hey bartender, I need another whiskey for me and another shot of tequila for this beautiful woman right here."

Tonia eyed him carefully as a sly grin spread across his face.

What do you think you're doing?

"What's the catch Stin? Why are you buying me drinks? What's up with you tonight?" Tonia asked. She didn't feel right being around him like this. With her supernatural powers, Tonia could hurt him within seconds. She didn't want to take that risk. She had better things to do with her time than hurting people.

"I just want to enjoy your company, what the hell? I don't have anything to do tonight. Lex is out at a party with his friends, and I'm just sitting here thinking about memories of how I got here and I don't want to grieve alone."

The sound of the glass hitting the counter broke the conversation. Tonia watched as Stin gripped the glass and downed the whiskey.

"So," he said. "Tell me about what happened to you in Africa. How did you end up being an orphan?"

Memories of her mother and father dying in their sleep, the gunshots, the men storming into the hut…It was too much for her to handle. Tonia stared at her drink. Her fingers glided to her chin, causing her to shift her focus to Stin again.

"My—uh…my parents were killed in the Congo in Africa. The people who killed them thought we were rich, that we had money stored somewhere in the hut we were living in." Tonia took a sip of the tequila. She felt the liquid burn her throat.

Anything to eliminate the pain.

"Let me guess they came in and shot everyone. Did you have any brothers or sisters?"

"I had one brother who they kidnapped. I tried to find him in the hut, but he wasn't there. I'll never forget the stench of my mother and father when I ran inside. They had been dead for hours." Another swig. Tonia's eyes averted to Stin's muscular arms bulging from his white shirt. Heat flamed between her thighs. She had to admit looking at him was a welcome distraction from all the pain she had endured within the last couple of hours…

Or years, depending on where the conversation was going.

"I'm sorry," he said. "I didn't know."

"A lot of people don't know. Well, maybe one." Tonia didn't want to say names. He should have known who that one person in her life was who didn't make her feel like a complete maniac all of the time even if she knew some of the things she did were nuts. If he didn't know who her best friend was then tough for him.

Stin took a couple of knocks with his knuckles on the counter before he spoke. "So how do you know this group kidnapped your brother?"

"I didn't see his body anywhere in the hut. I remember him telling my father in French that a group of guerrillas was trying to recruit him to join their army, but my brother wasn't interested. My parents wanted to keep my brother and me home to prevent us from getting killed, but it was no use. The army came in and killed my parents anyway. As for my brother…" Tonia trailed off. It had been years since she last saw her brother. She often wondered if she would ever find him after the raid.

"How old were you when this happened?"

"Eight," Tonia said. Tonia opened her mouth to yell at the bartender, but she must have read her mind as two more glasses darted across the counter, and the other two glasses disappeared. "My brother was thirteen when they kidnapped him. A part of me hoped they killed him too." There was no mistaking the anger coursing through her body as the acid bubbled inside her.

Her alter ego wanted to come out. She tried to protect her from the pain etched in her brain from the horrible images she envisioned in her mind. Another burn down her throat. She closed her eyes. Yes, she could finally feel herself getting drunk. This wasn't going to end up being suitable for her come morning.

"May I ask why?" he asked.

Tonia's eyes were starting to blur. The baby blues she adored were fading and twisting into a double vision so compelling, it almost knocked her down.

"Tonia?" She heard his voice, but it seemed so far away. Acid and heat burned her shoulders when Stin grabbed her and gave her a small shake. "Tonia?" he spoke again. Okay, so maybe she had a little too much to drink. Sure, she had a couple of drinks before but this? This was too much for her.

"Tonia, answer me. Are you okay?"

Tonia shook her head before she focused on where she was. Unfortunately, the physical contact between her and Stin only fueled the aching tension she had been trying to fight all night long. She blinked her eyes several times to knock out the drowsiness from the drink.

"Yes, I'm fine. I think the alcohol is starting to affect me." *That's not all it's affecting.* "I think I need to stop drinking now and just go home."

Stin nodded.

Tonia felt herself smile. "You know, I never thought I would say this, but I think you have the most gorgeous eyes I've ever seen." Tonia moved closer. Since Stin walked through the door, she hadn't thought about how she landed here in the first place. Was it a good thing? She wasn't sure.

She swore she could feel the intensity of his power through his chest as he gently grabbed her legs and swooped her into his arms.

"You've had way too much to drink tonight. I'm gonna take you home so you can get a good night's rest."

Rest. She needed it after the night she'd had. She closed her eyes. Rest seemed like the perfect idea…

***

This was not how he wanted the night to go.

It was supposed to end with Tonia lying naked in his bed and him being on top of her, desiring what he'd been dreaming about for several days. He'd wanted to avoid any contact with her at first because of her obsessive attitude with Ford. He knew she had a crush on him, but she let it take over her whole life. Stin remembered how much she used to stalk the guy before his fiancée Mandy came along. A part of him was grateful Ford had moved on with another woman and not Tonia.

In the end, they weren't perfect together.

At that time, he didn't care about her. He cared more about his best friend than anyone else on the team, even though Ford was also his boss. Correction: He cared about everyone else on the team except *her.* Stin couldn't stand her. He never liked the way she carried herself, like she was entitled to everything that ever crossed her path.

And he was always the one that had to put her in her place.

In some ways, he still didn't like her. He did, however, feel sorry for what she had gone through in Africa. He was moved by her story and wanted more. For the last couple of days, Stin had been going through a dry spell. The women he usually picked up from the bar were starting to feel the same. His one-night-stands were beginning to become boring.

The sex wasn't even that great for him anymore.

So now, he was standing here in a bar with the woman who he couldn't stand but was cradling her like a child after one too many drinks. He felt like the universe was laughing at him. Was this punishment for all the one-night stands he'd had in the past? If it was, then he'd survive. It hadn't been the first time women bared their soul to him after a few drinks. Difference was, they were still sober enough to give out sex and then pass out.

He felt Tonia stir in his arms. His body tingled as his eyes roamed down her chest. The outfit was showing enough cleavage to set his body and power on edge. He felt the bulge raging through his pants.

Can't have her this way. She has to be somewhat sober for you to sleep with her.

Stin grunted.

The only other option out of this whole situation was to take her home and call it a night. He sighed. The only way he could work off this energy was to surf the waves until his body grew tired. Hell, maybe it was what he needed to fight the desire swarming deep within his belly.

"Tonia?" he whispered softly. He didn't want her to freeze outside in the cold. It was only when one of the customers headed out the door that he realized it was daylight and the temperature was only sixty-two degrees. It was pointless to wake her up. Stin shifted.

"Would you like another drink, sir?" the bartender asked. *Must be new here*. Couldn't she see his guest was knocked out from all that drinks served earlier in the day?

"No, thanks. I'm going to call it a night. I need to take her home." Stin headed toward the door and kept heading straight. The glaciers collapsed into the ocean, turning the water that was once covered with ice and snow (his favorite superpower) into a lush aquamarine beauty. The leaves had grown back into their full form, making the island look even more like the ones he'd seen in the movies.

He always hated this time of the year, specifically for that reason.

After walking for what seemed like an eternity, Stin finally managed to come across Tonia's home. Though all of the homes were more like cabins than mansions, the Truson S.E.T. was allowed to do whatever they wanted to make the cabin stand out from the others. For that to happen, each of the members had to paint, remodel, and decorate within their own personal style. Hers was a lot fancier than most. The cabin was painted brown. A mailbox stating *Tonia Ojai, Truson S.E.T.* was written in blue writing.

Stop judging. Just drop the woman off and leave.

Problem was he needed a key to get in.

"Tonia?" he asked. He was taken aback by the sweet smell of tequila and strawberries. The sensation drove his erection into a sexual fury. This woman was doing things to him he didn't expect. A part of him didn't like it, but another part of him couldn't escape it.

He carefully leaned forward to set Tonia on her feet. She stumbled a few times to regain her balance before Stin finally helped her remain still. Her glassy light brown eyes stared back at him.

"I was enjoying the nap," she replied.

"Where are your keys?" Stin asked. His hands focused on her waist. Desire coursed through him again as he thought about how close he was to touching her ass.

"I—don't know. Can't—think," she said. His jaw clenched. He hoped his key would work, but it was unlikely. There was no other way to get in except for his powers. He lifted his hand toward the door. Tonia blocked his goal by pressing against him.

"You are so handsome. I never thought hating someone would be that hard."

He felt her breath on his skin. His alter ego roared.

Dude, pipe down. You haven't even had sex with her yet.

"Tonia, it's a little stuffy out here. Do you have the key to open the door? If not, we're going to have to use my powers…"

"I think—I think I left the card key back at the bar," she said. She giggled. "Did that make sense?"

Get her inside. At this point, they were going to be standing out there all day. She needed a warm place to sleep. Stin grabbed the handle and used ice to turn the knob until the knob fell to the ground. He reminded himself to replace the lock in the morning and carefully guided Tonia inside.

"You need to lie down and rest. You've had a little too much to drink."

Tonia massaged her fingers on the outside of Stin's shirt. Her fingers felt like silk. Heat flared through him.

Take her dude. You know you want to.

"Why can't I touch Ford like I can touch you?"

His heart dropped. *What a way to spoil the moment.* This was taking way too long. If he didn't get out of here soon, he might lose control. He picked Tonia up again and placed her on the couch.

Tonia grabbed his neck. His lips were inches apart from hers. The temperature increased. It felt like the room had reached a hundred degrees within the last few minutes. He couldn't sleep with her, not tonight.

But his body said otherwise. She leaned her head forward. All he could think about was him on top of her like he dreamed so many nights before. He had to let himself go to fulfill his desires. He didn't have to miss another opportunity now. She was in his face, ready and willing.

And drunk.

A gentle caress of her lips was all that was needed to change his mind. He took her mouth in his as the sweet sensations crawled through his abdomen. Her delicious tongue scraped his. He wanted more. He savaged the sweetness of her mouth as she ripped his shirt, exposing his chest. He needed to stop but he couldn't. He was in too deep now. There was no way of turning back. Stin let out a low groan as he fiddled with her dress. Once she was exposed, his mouth touched her beautiful nipples.

Stin caressed them one-by-one, forming invisible circles with his tongue. Tonia cried out as the nipples hardened like diamonds. Stin groaned. The sensations he felt were nothing compared to the other women he had sex with. Something was different about this one, but he couldn't put his finger on it.

"Stin, take me. I want to feel you. Make me forget, Stin," she mewed. Her voice was raw and full of passion, something in which he should have denied her. But it only made him want her more. Within seconds, his pants were undone, exposing his erection. Tonia purposefully grabbed it with her fingers and opened her mouth. There was no way she would do that sort of thing. Not now.

But he was wrong.

The warm liquid oozed all over his skin as she began sucking him. Stin leaned his head back as the blood rushed through his skull. The warmth reminded him of the ocean every time he decided to take a swim. Tension brewed inside him as she continued to go back and forth with her mouth.

Damn, she was good. So good he was about to—

"Tonia, I'm about to let go, and I don't—" She ignored him. "Tonia, I—" he tried to say it as loud as he possibly could, but he lost control. Her mouth let go before his hot liquid spilled onto her breasts. His whole body began to shake uncontrollably. He got up and held onto the armrest to control himself.

"Are you okay?" she asked.

He observed her dark-toned skin and light brown hair. Thoughts of her being unattractive and stuck up were replaced by how stunning she looked in her own skin. He couldn't lie to himself. He wanted her more than any other woman he'd desired before her.

"I'm fine," was all he could muster before he went through his pocket and pulled out a condom. He lay on top of Tonia and rammed himself inside her.

"Stin!"

He stared at her. Was it too much for her to handle? He should have thought about it before he pushed his weight on her, but he couldn't take it anymore. He needed to get all of his energy out.

"Am I hurting you?"

She shook her head no.

"Good." He continued. In and out. He could feel the moisture of her climax surrounding him as he dove deeper inside her. The feeling was intoxicating…way better than spending his nights' downing a glass of whiskey on a warm summer night. In and out. He felt himself coming to an explosion. He heard Tonia cry out again before he lost complete control.

And so did she.

Stin felt her walls closing in on him as he exploded inside her. Tonia's eyes twinkled before he managed to lie down on top of her. He caught his breath before he managed to lift his head to see if she was still awake. Surprisingly, she had fallen asleep and was snoring away on the couch. Stin shifted his weight by lifting himself up. It was getting late. He didn't feel like walking home. He mustered his strength and began searching for a nice place to sleep. He went to the first door and found Tonia's bed in a corner near the window of the cabin.

He collapsed on the bed, too exhausted to do anything else. He reminded himself he needed to pick up Lex from his friend's birthday party tomorrow. Then, maybe he and Lex could spend some quality time together surfing the waves on the island. Stin closed his eyes as he thought about them surfing, but a picture of Tonia interrupted his thoughts…

Let it happen. Stin's dreams took full course as he felt himself drifting off to sleep.

***

A knock at the door woke Tonia out of her sleep. She glanced around until she noticed the clock on the wall. Nine-thirty in the morning? It couldn't have been nine-thirty in the evening because she had arrived at ten 'o'clock at Nise's Bar and Grill.

Another knock followed.

"Tonia, are you in there? It's me, Ford. We need to talk." Tonia searched the room and found her silky black dress on the floor.

"Tonia?"

"I'm coming," she said. She grabbed the dress off of the floor and straightened the wrinkles out before she opened the door. Sure enough, her boss was standing in front of her, his auburn hair and dark brown eyes staring at her.

"Tonia, have you seen Stin? We need to talk to him, it's important." Tonia focused on the other three people standing behind him. She could tell by their body language something was wrong.

"What's going on Ford? Is everything okay?" Tonia watched as the woman stepped forward and pointed her finger behind her.

"That's him! That's the one that killed my daughter."

CHAPTER TWO

"Whoa lady, I don't know what you're talking about. I didn't murder anyone."

The woman lurched forward, causing Tonia to take a few steps back.

"How dare you lie about such a thing? We have proof you were the one who sank your jaws into my Jojo!"

Stin stared at the woman as she tossed the photo at him. The picture landed on the floor.

"I don't know what you're---"

Ford cut him off.

"I know what you are going to say, Stin. You don't have to repeat yourself." Ford came inside and stood in-between Stin and the unnamed woman. Stin picked up the photo off of the floor.

"Before we go any further, I think now would be the appropriate time to introduce ourselves. Stin and Tonia, these are three members of a group known as the Hammerhead Squad." Ford extended his hand. "This is Blake, leader of the Hammerhead Squad." The man was short and bald. He didn't seem like he would pose a threat to anyone.

Stin scoffed. A hammerhead versus an orca? He could take him down any day of the week. His alter ego stirred. Apparently, he agreed with his statement.

"This is Blake's wife, Jessica. She's second-in-command of the Hammerhead Squad. The last one to your left is Gio. He's the Hammerhead's top bodyguard."

"Why are they here?" Tonia asked.

"Because Stin is responsible for my daughter's death," Jessica said, pointing to him.

Stin stood in front of her.

"I don't know what's going on here, but I don't like what you are insinuating, especially when it comes to me," Stin said.

Ford cleared his throat.

"All right everyone, let's take a deep breath and calm down. I know this is a tough situation for the Hammerhead Squad, but I think we can easily resolve this by clarifying what's going on," Ford said.

"Well, I think that this woman just clarified it by accusing me of killing her daughter, which I had nothing to do with." Stin felt Tonia's eyes on him before she cut back to Ford.

"Ford, what's going on here?" Stin knew but needed to hear Ford repeat it for Tonia's sake.

"Stin is being accused of murder." Ford paused. "They have reason to believe Stin is responsible for their daughter's death." Ford walked over and took a seat on the couch. "I think maybe we should settle this in a calm and peaceful manner without accusations."

"You Ormans were never fair," Blake snarled. "I don't see why we decided to have this meeting with you when we should have just killed Stin on the spot and left already."

Stin lurched forward, his alter ego rising to the surface. Blake had no right to accuse him of such a crime—not without proof.

Stin was ready for a fight.

"Take it easy. If you are going to continue to insult my team then perhaps we shouldn't have this meeting." Ford turned to Stin. "Stin, where were you two nights ago? Do you remember anything at all?"

"Yeah, I remember. I was out glacier surfing."

"In the middle of the night?" Jessica piped in. "That seems a little strange for a guy to be out surfing alone, don't you think?"

"And isn't it strange that a woman like you should mind your own damn business?" Stin replied.

Jessica moved forward, hell-bent on proving just how powerful she was. Stin had no doubt she was powerful, but so was he.

If it was a war she wanted, then she picked the right person.

"Enough!" Ford barked. "There was a photo you picked up?"

"Here it is," Tonia said. She turned it upside down. "No matter how many ways I've looked at it, there is no denying the picture is authentic."

Stin stood behind her to see the photo. There was a picture of an orca attacking a hammerhead with its mouth. Stin couldn't see anything except the orca and the hammerhead attacking each other.

"It's a picture of an orca and a hammerhead fighting. Do you know how many times that happens in a day in the Arctic ocean? Besides, we only attack our enemies once they attack us. That's always been our rule."

"Well, you won't get away with breaking the law on our side of town," Blake piped in. "We know you killed our daughter, and you're going to pay for what you've done."

Stin watched Tonia as she stared at the picture again. Her mouth dropped. Oh, how he wanted to kiss that mouth again…

Cut it out, dude. She was a one-night stand, remember? Nothing more.

"What's wrong?" Stin asked, breaking the silence in the room.

"There's a blue marking under the orca's belly. Look."

Stin took the picture and looked at it. He wiped the blue marking with his thumb to make sure the image wasn't colored in. The marking never moved.

His heart slammed into his chest. There was no way possible he could have killed her. The image had to be a fake.

"I guess you're starting to believe us now, huh?" Jessica said. "How does it feel to know you're responsible for killing a sixteen-year-old minor?"

"Wait a minute. This might be Stin in the photo, but who's to say that the hammerhead is your daughter?" Tonia squinted at the photo. "I'm sorry, what was your daughter's name again?"

"Jojo Hammerhead. Our daughter was going to take over the entire organization once my wife and I decided not to run the business anymore. That is until you decided to take her away from us by attacking her for no reason."

"I disagree with that statement," Ford piped in. "I will admit that all of us on the Truson Super Elite Team have a special marking based on the powers we obtain through the Animan three-hundred. The marking indicates the difference between a Truson team member and regular orcas." Ford extended his hand, an indication he needed to see the photo again. Stin was more than happy to give it to him.

"This photo may have been him, but we still have no idea what happened or who provoked who."

"You're out of your damn mind," Blake said, inching forward.

Stin's alter ego started clawing at him again. Stin and Tonia stood beside him in a flash, ready for a fight. "There is no way of justifying killing a sixteen-year-old girl. She's a minor."

"I think this is a waste of time," Gio said, breaking his silence.

Stin had to admit he had forgotten about him since the whole meeting began.

Apparently, so did the others.

All eyes focused on Gio as he rose up from the couch. He was a heavy-set man: broad shoulders, short curly black hair and a body that could rip his suit at any time—but that wasn't enough to intimate him in the least. He dealt with more than his fair share of enemies and Gio was no different.

"Stin is not going to admit to anything. Even if he's guilty, he won't admit it. Ford makes an excellent point. How do we know if the hammerhead in the photo is really Jojo?"

Stin scoffed. Even their own bodyguard supported them. What kind of group was this?

"So now you're taking their side? What the hell is the matter with you? I pay you good money to guard us, and this is what I get?" Blake said.

"You know what? I've had enough of this. Everybody out!" Stin grabbed the photo and tore the picture in half. The picture hadn't even dropped to the floor before Blake showed his gun.

"My picture!" Jessica screamed. The woman scrambled to the floor and picked up the remaining pieces of the last images of her daughter. Stin could tell Ford wanted to be the mediator, but that all changed once Blake pulled out his gun.

"You're going to pay for that. If it was up to me right now…" Blake moved closer. Before Stin could blink, Tonia stepped in, knocking the gun out of his hand. Blake motioned toward the gun.

"I would be careful if I were you," she warned. Part of the gun was already disappearing due to the acid that flowed from her fingers.

"It's okay Blake. No one's going to be able to represent him anyhow. Without a lawyer, he's going straight to the death chair," Jessica said, reassuring her husband.

"Who said Stin doesn't have a lawyer?"

Stin focused on Tonia as her eyes changed from a light fiery green back to light brown. The intensity in her eyes still burned through his skin like a raging inferno.

"Are you saying you're going to represent him?" Ford asked.

Stin waited on her response. Did he sense hesitation on her part?

Tonia took a deep breath. "Yes, I'm going to represent him. I don't think he murdered Jojo."

That statement said it all.

Despite everything that had happened within the last twenty-four hours, Tonia believed his story—better, Tonia believed in *him.* Stin couldn't help but swell in pride as the thought sank in. He had never been in these types of situations before, but he had to admit it felt good that somebody besides his best friend believed in him for once. As much as the thought entertained him, it was short-lived when Jessica squinted at all three of them. She shook her head.

"You won't get away with this. You may have your stupid sidekick as your lawyer, but you won't get away with this. I'll make you pay."

"We heard your side of the story. You were able to speak your peace. Now it's time for you to leave."

Stin sensed the irritation in Ford's voice and stared at Ford's arms. His veins were turning into an orange glow that sprang to his shoulders.

If the Hammerheads weren't going to go out peacefully, the Truson Super Elite Team was going to show them what they were about, and he just so happened to be one of those people.

"Let's get out of here. The last thing we need is for this situation to get out of hand. We don't want this case to blow up in our faces," Gio said.

"And here I thought you were on our side. So disappointed," Tonia said and cocked her head to the side as Jessica ran forward to grab her. The moment she wanted to shout; her head contorted into an odd shape. Her skin began to stretch out in unusual proportions. It took Stin a few moments to analyze her before he finally realized what was happening: She was turning into a hammerhead before his very eyes, something in which he thought was damn near impossible to do.

Luckily, Gio and Blake were able to grab her before the situation got worse. Stin admitted to himself he almost felt sorry for Jessica. She had to be in a lot of pain after losing her daughter. In his defense, he was willing to do whatever it took to protect himself and his team from harm,

And that included Tonia.

"We'll see you at the trial," Ford announced as their bodyguard pushed them toward the entranceway. Tonia did the honors by slamming the door in their faces.

"I can't believe you brought them into my house, Ford. What were you thinking?"

"I wanted to allow both of them to share their stories. I was hoping to reach some conclusion or agreement before any of this went to trial." Ford shifted his weight. "I didn't realize it was going to be *that* intense." Ford's cell interrupted the conversation.

"Hello? Hi Sweetheart, is everything okay?…Yeah, I just finished up the meeting, and I'm heading over there right now…" Stin gave a nod to Ford before he headed out the door. The muscles stung in Stin's body as his alter ego tore at his skin. The threat was officially over, but he still couldn't understand why his alter ego became so restless.

"Well, this was an exciting morning," Tonia said. She shrugged her shoulders. "I would offer you breakfast, but it might take a while. Sometimes when I cook, I like to cook for an army."

Stin smiled. As much as he'd enjoyed last night, he knew he couldn't ask her to do anything more. A part of him felt guilty about last night, considering the condition she was in. Besides, he didn't know if he had any more room in his life for a relationship considering he was now the legal guardian of a sixteen-year-old. After what happened last year, he didn't dare let Lex Stevenson anywhere near her.

Yet another reason why you two shouldn't be together…

He had to let her go. When it came down to her and Lex, Lex had to be his top priority. His job was to protect him at all costs. If that meant giving her up as his attorney and staying as far away from her as possible, then so be it. He didn't like the idea, but it had to be done whether he liked it or not…

***

Neither one of them moved from their position. Tonia felt stupid staring Stin down like candy, especially when they were almost under attack by another round of enemies planning on destroying the team once again. Giddiness escaped through her veins when she knocked the gun out of Blake's hands. She could quickly tell by their behavior they had no powers whatsoever. All they were good for was transforming into another animal and letting the animal do all the dirty work.

They were nothing but a bunch of cowards. They didn't hold the powers that the Truson S.E.T. had. If she didn't believe in giving Stin or any of the members a 'fair trial,' she would have killed them right then. How dare they come into her home and accuse her of being a sidekick to an attack she knew nothing about? If she couldn't tell the difference between the thousands of hammerheads that roamed the earth, how could they?

Something screamed set-up. Tonia felt it. However, she couldn't prove anything based on a gut feeling. She needed evidence, and so far it was only Stin's word against the Hammerhead Squad.

What to do?

"Tonia." That cool sexy voice brought her back to why this all happened in the first place. She hadn't meant to have a one-night stand with someone she couldn't stand. He was handsome, and he did have some of the most gorgeous baby blues she's ever seen, but last night was as far as it should have gone. Representing him was going to be too much on her part.

"Tonia?" Her gaze landed on his face. The intensity in his eyes told her he was struggling with something, but Tonia couldn't understand what.

"Look Stin, I don't know what just happened now but—"

"—Tonia please. I have to say this before you go any further," Stin said, cutting her off.

"Well, I think that what I have to say is important too. It's way more important than what you have to say."

"I doubt that very much since I've decided I do not want you representing me for this trial."

Tonia paused. She swallowed. That was what she wanted to say. Frankly, she should have been relieved that he was the one who said it.

"What did you say?" She felt the powers growing.

"Tonia, I thank you for believing in me when it came to the accusations and for defending me against the Hammerheads, and even though I shouldn't have taken advantage of you last night, the sex was great, but we can't do it ever again. I'm sorry."

Tonia couldn't move or speak at that moment. The words echoed in her brain like a wrecking ball. All this time, she felt like a fool. He had taken advantage of her at the bar. He got her to tell him about her biggest secrets, including talking about what happened back in her home country of Africa. Then if that wasn't enough, he decided to have sex with her and then dump her like she meant nothing to him. Like all of the women before her, she was another one on his to-do list.

How could you have been so stupid?

"Get out" was all she could muster. If she said anymore, there was going to be acid shooting out of her mouth and landing on Stin's face. She remembered the last time it happened and how much she'd regretted it. This time was going to be much different.

"Tonia—"

"Get out Stin! Get out of my house right now, or else the Hammerheads won't be your only concern." She stared at the lamp nearby. With one swift movement of her hand, acid flew out in a flash, sending the contents through the table and down into the floor below.

First warning.

Next time it will be his head.

“I’m leaving,” he said. He reached for the knob before facing her again. “Hope you feel better.”

Tonia squinted. Before she could send out her next attack, Stin was gone. She heard his footsteps as he walked out the door. Then nothing, leaving Tonia alone with her thoughts.

Usually, she was okay with being alone. This time was different.

Her alter ego stirred again. She was getting restless and knew what she needed to relieve the stress. She searched the bedroom and the living room until she was able to locate her cell at the edge of the couch. She became alarmed when the strong scent of what smelled like body wash invaded her nostrils.

Only then did she realize Stin had slept in her bed while she passed out drunk. That bastard! He took advantage of her like all the others and dared to sleep in her bed afterward. Tonia's powers ripped through her fingers again. She jumped back, the phone burning in her hand.

You need a break. Go out and get you some fresh air.

Moreover, she could see if Su-Lee was at home. She wasn’t familiar with Su-Lee's schedule, considering how she was the computer tech behind the Truson S.E.T. operation. Regardless, she needed to find her to get the emotional anger boiling inside her off her chest. The only way she could do it was having a conversation with her best friend. Tonia picked up the phone again and dialed

Su-Lee's number. She was just about to hang up when it stopped ringing. Tonia exhaled.

"Hello?"

"Su-Lee? It's me, Tonia. Are you busy?"

"No. I was asleep but it's okay. Why? What's up?"

Tonia hesitated on what she wanted to say. She didn't want Su-Lee to get the wrong impression. Who knew what her reaction was going to be once she found out what happened between her and Stin?

"Are you still there?"

"Yeah, I'm here."

"Wait a minute, I was looking for you last night. Where were you?" Su-Lee asked.

Great, now she had to tell her the truth.

"I went to a bar last night. I was pretty upset about Ford and everything, so I just decided to get away from it all." Tonia replayed the scene in her head of the night the group gave out warm wishes to the two newest members of the Truson Super Elite Team, with one of them being a woman she despised greatly. Tonia honestly thought that if Mandy hadn't come along in the first place, she would have had a chance to explore the relationship with Ford. That was then, this is now.

"Then what happened? Is everything okay? You sound a little upset."

"Hell, I was mad when I arrived at the bar. Everything would have been just fine if I had let myself out of the bar *alone.*"

"Meaning?" Silence. Could she even say what really happened last night without cringing?

"I don't know what happened except seeing Stin sitting right next to me and asking me about my personal life and me babbling about what happened to me back in the Congo."

"Wow! You told him about what happened to your family?"

"Yup."

"And your brother too?"

"Yup."

"What about you getting AIDS? Did you tell him about that too?" she asked.

"We didn't get that far." Memories of her being raped and sold for sex invaded her mind. Even though the virus left her system the moment she became an Orman, it had been a long time since she'd thought about what happened and didn't want to relive the memories from her past.

"I made a fool of myself by getting drunk and passing out in Stin's arms."

"I can't believe it. I thought I would never see the day where you and Stin would be hanging out at a bar at night. Were you two hanging out at Nise's Bar and Grill?" Su-Lee asked.

"Of course we were. Nise wasn't working there."

"Did Stin follow you?" Su-Lee pressed.

These were questions she hadn't thought about. There was no time to think about every little detail. The only way Tonia could break the interrogation was just to let herself vent her frustration before she ended her day by taking a quick swim to get her mind off of recent events.

"Stin and I slept together. We had a one-night stand, and now I'm regretting it because that's all we are, and that's all we are ever going to be, and I was stupid enough to fall for his baby blue eyes and then the next thing I knew, we're kissing and touching each other, and I woke up on the couch while he slept in my bed." More silence. "Su-Lee, are you still there?"

"Yaaaaaaay!" Tonia heard some static over the phone before she heard Su-Lee's voice again. "It's finally happened. I didn't believe it was going to happen, but it did. I'm so proud of you right now."

"Proud? How can you possibly say you're proud of me when the man practically told me he didn't want to have anything to do with me? I can't believe he dismissed me like that even after I decided to represent him in court…"

"Wait a minute, you're losing me here. What court? I don't understand."

"I'm surprised Ford didn't mention anything to you about it. Stin has been accused of murder." Tonia drank a few sips of water.

"And who is accusing him of murder?"

"The Hammerhead Squad," Tonia replied. The warm liquid was a welcome change from the many drinks she'd had last night.

"Those stupid people? That group is notorious for lying and backstabbing. I wouldn't believe a word that comes out of their mouths. Who do they claim he murdered?"

"A sixteen-year-old girl name Jojo Hammerhead," Tonia said. "I'll tell you more about it if you're up to going out for a swim in the ocean." Tonia put the glass away and headed toward the door. She couldn't fight her alter ego anymore. It was tearing away at her skull.

She needed to get out.

"I'm on my way," was all she heard Su-Lee say before she managed to toss her phone aside and dive into the ocean below just as her alter ego was taking form.

CHAPTER THREE

Stin recalled the conversation over again in his brain. He wanted to be okay with how he'd left things. It seemed only fair that he told her the truth before she got her hopes up of their one-night stand turning into something more. He couldn't let her think that way. Stin Vanderson didn't do relationships—they were too complicated.

So why did he feel like an asshole for telling her how he felt?

She had every right to be angry with him. He did tell her he didn't want her representing him as his lawyer when it came to this murder case. Stin remembered Ford telling him Tonia was one of the most prolific lawyers on the island. She made a reputation out of defending countless victims who had been accused of all sorts of crimes, including murder. Stin managed to put all of that aside as he approached the doorway.

He wondered if Lex had had a good time hanging out with his friends last night. He didn't even want to think about the other things that might have possibly gone on while he was with Tonia. Stin put on his brightest smile as the woman opened the door.

"Hello madam, I'm here to pick up Lex?"

"About time you showed up," the woman barked. "Lex, your father's here to pick you up."

Okay, don't like her.

The woman stepped a few inches back as Lex got in front of her. His hair was ruffled, his clothes were dirty and partially torn from the waist down, and his eyes were hidden behind a unique pair of shades to block out the horrible rays of the sun. Despite his efforts, Stin couldn't figure out how to cover the patches that revealed his skin. All it took was a few minutes outside for his skin to burn like fire.

"Hey," Lex said, lifting his head up to greet him.

"Hey," Stin greeted him in return. "You ready to go?"

"Of course he is. Can you just hurry up and get him out of my entranceway? I have a million other things to do today and babysitting him—" The woman pointed her finger at Lex. "—is not on my agenda for today." There it was again. Stin sensed the ice tracking through his veins. His alter ego roared inside.

"Excuse me, I don't think you know who I am, but I'm part of an excellent team of folks that is likely to kick your ass if you so much as insult us." He paused. "I would suggest you don't insult Lex again or else you're going to regret it dearly." Stin focused on Lex. Lex was bobbing down to the other side of the island. "Have a great day." Stin flew off the porch and jogged toward Lex.

"Lex!" he called out. Stin thought it might slow him down but instead, he did the opposite. Heat suddenly radiated through his skin. This was something Stin had to avoid at all costs. The sun was only going to make his powers weaken.

Just like Lex.

He suddenly remembered the holes in Lex's pants and jogged faster to catch up to him. Stin picked up his feet and called Lex out for the second time. His feet began to slow down, but he didn't stop walking entirely.

"Lex, are you okay? You seem upset," Stin said, waiting on his response. Lex turned and blocked him from his path.

"Why did you boast about being a part of the Truson S.E.T.?" he asked.

"Well, I'm going to do whatever I possibly can to protect you. You should know that by now."

Lex searched the other direction. "Yeah, but why? I'm not your biological son. I'm Vernon Stevenson's rotten bastard."

"Hey dude, don't say that about yourself. Your father was the bastard, not you. What's going on with you today? Did you have a great time at the party?" His behavior seemed a little off. Usually, Lex would be happy to see him or even suggest going out for a swim in thc ocean, but not today. Something was different.

"I did until one of my friends saw you with Tonia last night."

Dammit, even on this island he wasn't allowed privacy. First, it was the Hammerhead Squad spying on him to accuse him of something he didn't commit, and now it was one of Lex's friends. Stin wondered if he was ever going to get time alone while he stayed on the island.

"What were you doing hanging out with her?" Lex asked. Stin's first reaction was to tell him that whatever went on between Tonia and him was their business and that he needed to stop asking questions. But since the Hammerhead Squad arrived a few hours ago, his previous thought was taken off the table. If he ever changed his mind about Tonia representing him, then Lex needed to know.

"She's helping me out of a situation."

"What kind of situation?"

"One that involves me being accused of something I didn't do." He tried to think about what he wanted to say without giving away too much information. He didn't want to worry Lex about something that might possibly happen.

"Look, I know you two weren't on the best of terms and I can't say I blame you for being angry with her but trust me, she's doing something extraordinary for the both of us."

"I can't see how that's possible considering what she has done to both of us, not just me." Lex shook his head. "Whatever, do what you want. I have to go and change before I start to burn up in flames." Lex picked up the pace. Stin followed him.

The lesion on Lex's skin was growing at a slow pace, but it was enough for Stin to be concerned. As Stin was about to push Lex into the water to protect him, a massive surge of pain escaped inside, causing his entire body to react as he felt himself fall to the ground. The world had spun for only a few seconds before he managed to turn and see who was bold enough to attack him. Stin didn't even have a chance to breathe as the attackers struck again, this time in the face. The liquid that came from the attacker's knuckles burned him and caused a wave of fatigue he couldn't shake off.

What the hell is going on? What is this stuff? A gush of wind went past him before the darkness crept over him. The attacker was fading from his vision as he felt himself floating from reality. Stin took one final glance at Lex, who had turned into rocks and stones before Stin closed his eyes for the last time, the darkness consuming his soul.

***

Stin wasn't going to die. Not now, not ever.

Those thoughts stayed with Lex as he continued to throw rocks and stones at the intruder. Just who exactly was that clown? Whoever it was, they weren't going to stand a chance against him. Lex couldn't believe the nerve of this person attacking Stin in the middle of the day. Didn't they have boundaries when it came to something like this? Who cared? If they didn't respect boundaries, then Lex was going to make whoever it was respect them. Lex continued the attack on the intruder but had to give the intruder credit for putting up a good fight.

The intruder did its absolute best to avoid the blows Lex was offering with his powers. The intruder made a few sneak attacks, but Lex bounced back even before the intruder had a chance to overpower him. He loved the power and glory when it came to his supernatural strength, but his arms were tired, and he needed to get to Stin as soon as possible. Every time he or she inched closer, Lex shot out another rock, this time hitting the intruder in the chest.

War's over.

The intruder fell backward onto the ground. Lex let out a sigh of relief before being disappointed once again when the intruder pushed himself up and continued to hold his chest. Lex waited on the next attack. The man coughed up shots of blood before he squinted at Lex.

"You may have defeated me now *Lex*," he said between breaths, "but I've come here with a warning: The Hammerheads will be back to finish the job." Those last words stuck in Lex's mind as the intruder collapsed on the ground. Lex waited for him to get back up again. When his body continued to lie still, Lex rushed to Stin's aid, his mind racing as he asked himself what kind of damage the attacker might have done to cause such an injury.

"Stin! Stin, I'm here! Stin, wake up!" Lex shook him as hard as he could, but nothing happened. Purplish green slime covered his face and neck. Lex leaned closer. The horrible smell was unlike anything he had ever smelled in his life. It made him cringe.

Stop wasting time.

Lex grabbed his cell and dialed the number to the Truson Headquarters. If this was the only way to save Stin's life, then that was what he'd have to do. Stin wasn't going to die. Lex already had two people in his life who were gone, he couldn't take losing a third.

"C'mon Stin! I need you. You're all I have dude. You have to wake up."

***

She shouldn't have done it. She knew what the consequences were. After all, this was the same man whom she hated with every fiber of her being. Besides those gorgeous eyes and sexy short blond locks, Stin was nothing more to her than a bad one-night stand walking on two legs. Everything about this man was telling her to run in another direction and avoid the pending case looming over his head.

Su-Lee was an added comfort to the situation. She congratulated her on finally moving on but would have preferred her being with someone else besides Stin.

"I thought you would have known by now how Stin is, considering all the women he screwed from Nise's Bar and Grill," Su-Lee said.

"He took advantage of me while I was drunk. I should have kicked him out of my house then but nooo, I had to go and do something stupid by saying I would be the one representing him in court after the Hammerheads accused him of murder. What the hell was I thinking?" Tonia asked. She grabbed the towel nearby and wiped off the moisture dripping down her legs. Changing into her alter ego with her best friend was just the thing she'd needed to vent and get her mind off of things.

"You were thinking about protecting him from being killed. Do you think he is guilty of what the Hammerheads are accusing him of?"

"Despite that picture of an orca having a blue marking underneath its belly and attacking a hammerhead underwater? Yeah, I still think he's innocent." Su-Lee pointed to another towel nearby. Tonia tossed the towel. Su-Lee wiped herself off.

"How did they manage to take a picture like that underwater anyway?" Su-Lee asked. "They had already shifted when the attack happened."

"I know." Tonia shrugged. "Frankly, I'm done with trying to figure all of this stuff out. He doesn't want me to represent him, fine. Let someone else do it. I'm just upset he dismissed me like I was just some whore he found in the street."

"But you're not," Su-Lee said, putting her hand on Tonia's shoulder. "You're a survivor, Tonia. You went through the most terrifying and devastating event in your life." Su-Lee paused. Her eyes drifted to the other side of the island before she focused her attention on Tonia. "Does he know about how you contracted AIDS and died in the Congo?"

"No." *Thank God.* "If I had told him that, then the situation would probably have been far worse."

"Or better," Su-Lee said.

Before Tonia could attest to her statement, Su-Lee's cell phone rang.

"Hello? Yeah, I'm just hanging out with Tonia, why? Is there something wrong? You need technical support on it?" Tonia knew where this was going. Their short conversation about Stin and his rude behavior was coming to an end. Back to business as usual. Su-Lee clicked off. "I have to…"

"Yes, I know. Do they need my assistance for anything?"

"No. This is just technical stuff. I'll talk to you later, okay?"

Tonia nodded. Now she had to figure out what she was going to do for the rest of the day…which landed her at her desk writing an opening statement to Stin's trial.

He had made it very clear he didn't want her help. On top of that, Stin made her feel like she was just another woman he could dispose of. Considering how long she had been on the island, she should have known better than to sleep with Stin Vanderson. She should have known better than to write an opening statement despite Stin's comment.

So why was she sitting here like a fool about to write something she knew she wasn't going to use?

A sound interrupted her thoughts. It wasn't until the second ring that she realized it was her cell. She glanced at the number and paused. She didn't recognize it but decided to answer. "Hello?"

"Tonia, it's me, Ford."

Tonia waited for some sort of reaction to Ford's voice. No heart beating out of her chest, no tingling sensations she used to get every time he said a word to her—nothing. All of those feelings had disappeared.

"Tonia, are you still there?"

"Yes. I'm here, boss. What do you need?" she asked.

"I just called to let you know Stin is in the hospital. Apparently, he suffered some sort of attack from an unknown intruder. We need you to come down here right away."

An attack? Tonia couldn't help but picture Stin punching and shoving some guy in the face and torso. He didn't seem like the type to get attacked by anyone.

"When did this happen?"

"A couple of hours ago. I think you should really come down and see this."

"No offense Ford, but Stin made it very clear he doesn't want to see me. We haven't been on the same page when it comes to me representing him at this trial," Tonia replied.

"Tonia, whatever Stin says about not needing a lawyer for this trial—screw it. The reason why I came to you is because I knew you would be the right person for the job. Despite whatever Stin says, he needs you, Tonia. Now, get down here and see what's going on."

Tonia was taken aback by the tone in his voice.

"So, I guess that's an order, huh?"

"Yes."

She waited on the physical emotions she used to feel whenever he became so demanding. It was the kind of thing that used to turn her on at a moment's notice. So far, that wasn't happening.

"I'll be there soon," was all she could muster before she heard a dial tone at the other end of the line. She hung up and decided to follow her boss's orders by getting dressed and investigating what was going on.

That was the least she could do

***

Tonia didn't hesitate to go through the double doors of the hospital. She surprised herself when she walked up to the second floor and found Stin lying in the hospital bed. Ford wasn't exaggerating when he told her Stin had been beaten severely. His face was full of red and purple gashes followed by crystals—green crystals—that Tonia didn't recognize.

"What happened?" Tonia asked, examining Stin's face. "Why are there bruises on his face? We are supposed to heal ourselves whenever we are attacked. Why are the bruises still there?"

"We think somebody used a special potion to attack Stin. Whatever it was, Stin is allergic to it," Ford said.

Tonia processed the information before she managed to speak again.

"Wait a minute, Stin has allergies? I was under the impression that once we were Ormans, we are no longer vulnerable to those illnesses?"

Ford shrugged and folded his arms across his chest.

"It depends on the situation. Usually, our bodies can fight off anything but in Stin's case, whatever materials they used caused his face to break out like…" Ford cut himself off and extended his hand toward the bed.

Tonia knew by the expression on his face he wanted to rip someone's head off.

"Has he woken up yet?" Tonia hoped that changing the subject would calm Ford down for the time being. The last thing the Truson S.E.T. needed was to retaliate for what happened to Stin since Stin was now a suspect in a murder trial. Ford cleared his throat.

"No, not yet. I'm waiting for him to wake up so he can tell me what happened."

"You don't need him to wake up for you to figure out what happened," a familiar voice echoed in the room. Both Tonia and Ford focused their attention toward the door. Tonia's heart sank into her chest as she saw the dark scratches escalating down Lex's arms. A bruise sat on his right cheek.

"I can tell you what happened." Tonia walked toward Lex, reaching out to touch the scratches, but she caught herself. What the hell was she doing? Lex hated her. He had every reason to.

"Spill Lex. Are you okay?" Ford leaned over to inspect the scratches on his arm.

"I'm fine. Whoever it was wanted to kill me but didn't get the opportunity to finish the job." Tonia watched Lex's eyes roam from her to Stin. "Did Stin wake up yet?"

"That's what we're waiting on," Tonia replied.

Lex squinted. The intense stare made her shift her weight. Memories of her spewing out harsh words to Lex and his two friends invaded her mind.

Forget about the past. Focus on what you need to do.

"Tonia, can I talk to you for a second?"

Tonia straightened herself up and followed Lex outside of Stin's door.

"What were you and Stin talking about earlier? Stin said something about him being in some sort of trouble, but he never mentioned what kind of trouble he might be in," Lex said. Tonia processed Lex's statement and thought about the intention Stin might have had when it came to keeping Lex in the dark about the pending murder trial looming over his head. There was no way Tonia wanted to be responsible for Lex going out and doing something stupid to protect Stin. Stin would never forgive her for letting him know the truth and being partially responsible for Lex's obnoxious behavior. Hell, she probably wouldn't forgive herself for supporting such behavior.

Tonia contemplated what she should do while Lex leaned against the wall with his hands in his pockets, waiting on her response. Even in the hospital, he wore his black hoodie over his head to block himself from the rays of fluorescent lights glowing throughout the building. The tiniest speck of light would quickly make his skin feel like he'd been sunburned.

"What did Stin tell you?"

"That he's in a lot of trouble and that you might be the one to help him out of it."

"Well, if that's what he told you, then I agree."

Lex shrugged.

"But that's not telling me anything. I don't understand why he would go to you of all people to help him when he hates your guts."

The insult stung Tonia in the chest. Usually, she wouldn't be affected by something like this, but somehow she was. Why should she care about what Lex thought? He was nothing but a sixteen-year-old orphaned kid who just so happened to have powers beyond his control. As far as Tonia knew, he was trying to find a place to belong in their world, and it just so happened that Stin was the one who took on that type of responsibility.

Who was she to come in-between that?

"Actually, Ford extended the offer to help Stin out of a tough situation he's in right now but if you want to know the whole story, I think you should talk to Stin about what's going on." There. She didn't want to be blamed for anything out of turn, especially when it came to Lex. She had enough problems to deal with.

Tonia moved her head to the side and caught Ford gawking at her again. She knew something was on his mind, but he didn't want Lex to hear any of it. Frankly, she'd had enough of talking to both of them. The air of the hospital in addition to the sick patients roaming back and forth, looking for a place of solitude was starting to get to her.

Pictures of Stin's bruised face entered her mind. She felt her emotions escalating throughout her body. Whoever did that to him was surely going to pay for that mistake, but now wasn't the time. A part of her wanted to reach out and touch him, to let him know she was still here despite his behavior toward her.

It would be best if you walk away now. No commitments.

Frankly, she couldn't understand why she cared in the first place. Her best bet would have been to walk away and not look back.

Doing it as a favor for Ford, remember?

"Lex, why don't you stay here with Stin in his room? I'm going to need someone to watch over him in case he wakes up."

"No problem." Lex's eyes focused on Tonia. "I think I need some answers about what's going on anyway."

Direct hit. Do not give into it. Lex turned his back and flopped down in the seat closest to Stin as Ford ushered her out into the hallway a few feet away from Stin's hospital doors.

"I think we should find out who did this and make sure they don't get away with it. Su-Lee got some DNA from one of the nurses in the hospital and is scanning it now."

Tonia couldn't take her eyes off of Stin's doorway, hoping Lex would come and say that he was awake.

"I need you to help Su-Lee find him."

"It's not a good idea," Tonia finally said. "He's on trial for murder. The last thing Stin needs is more ammunition against him. Doing a full out war with this individual will draw more attention to Stin."

"So what am I supposed to do? Just sit back and watch whoever did this have the opportunity to do it again? I'm the—"

"—Leader of the Truson Super Elite Team. It's your job to protect us. I get it, Ford. This type of thing infuriates you, but it's not a good idea and as much as you hate it, the best thing for you to do is nothing."

"She's right," a voice said, breaking the conversation. "If you do anything now, it will only make Stin look more guilty."

Tonia cringed on the inside as she recognized the voice flowing through the hallway. She glared at the woman who walked up and put a delicate hand on Ford's shoulder. She gently pecked Ford on the cheek.

Great, what a way to rub it in.

"What are you doing here? I thought you were going to be at home grading papers?"

"She's grading papers? I thought you were running the Truson School for Shapeshifters?" Tonia asked. She shouldn't have asked that question. Who was she to ask questions after Ford clearly told her he only saw her as a friend and nothing more?

"I decided to take a break and come see you, and from the looks of things, I'm glad I did." Mandy turned to Tonia. "Looks like I was in the middle of you going postal on some guy who attacked Stin. Is he okay?"

"He's not waking up," Ford replied. "I was talking to Tonia to work out a plan and figure out who was behind all of this."

"I think I should go," Tonia said before the conversation went any further. She walked past Ford and put a hand on his shoulder. "Please don't do anything that would jeopardize his trial. We can't afford any more reasons for Stin to look guilty."

Ford nodded.

Tonia wasn't sure if he understood or was just nodding to avoid a confrontation, but she didn't care.

Despite what Stin stated to her before the attack, he still needed a lawyer. Despite the fact that she hated his guts, Tonia still wanted to represent him.

How crazy was that?

CHAPTER FOUR

Stin kept hearing the sounds over and over again—the water crashing against the waves. The iceberg collapsing and falling deep within the ocean floor. The sun shone brightly, his skin feeling like peels of an orange.

"It's about time you woke up," a familiar voice said. The sun was a constant reminder that summer had officially arrived on the island, and it was here to stay for the next few months. A part of him should have been happy the sun was out and about—it had given him the perfect excuse to go out and do one of his favorite activities: Surfing. But he preferred it more when the sun wasn't out the whole day. Too sunny for his taste.

"How are you feeling?" was the next question that spilled out of Ford's mouth. Usually, he was grateful to see his best friend during times like these, but this time there was someone else he wanted attention from and it wasn't him.

"Like shit. What the hell happened to me?" he asked. His eyes searched the room as his alter ego roared in protest. "How long have I been like this?"

"A while. We were worried you weren't going to wake up. Some guy attacked you—attacked both of us—while we were walking home," Lex replied. The images slowly flooded back, but there was one thing he was unsure about.

"What about Tonia? Is she okay?" He held his breath. He couldn't remember if Tonia had been by his side and if she had, there was a possibility she could have been injured from the attack or worse.

He felt his abilities strengthen. The ice ran through his veins. *If anyone hurts her, I'll kill him.*

"Tonia's fine. As a matter of fact, she came by to see you earlier, but you were still out of it." Stin felt his heart drop.

A part of him was relieved she wasn't in the attack, but another part of him still wanted her to stick around and apologize for her behavior earlier. Thoughts of the conversation they shared together shuffled through his mind.

That's probably the reason why she didn't stay you ass.

"Is she here now?" *Desperate much?*

"No, she's not. She left a few hours ago."

Stin shifted his focus on Lex. The intensity in Lex's eyes told him how much he didn't like him asking about her.

"Do you remember who did this to you?" Ford asked.

His alter ego heightened again. Bits and pieces of the attack invaded his mind, but there were no facial features.

"No, it happened too fast. Couldn't see anything. I wish I could find out who did this to me, though. I'll give him a piece of my power he won't forget."

Ford chuckled.

Despite the fact his mind was elsewhere, hearing Ford laugh again was always a welcoming experience. Stin tried to remember the last time they hung out together as buddies, and the only time he could think of was the celebration of his girlfriend Mandy and his adoptive son Lex being the newest members of the Truson S.E.T.

That was a week ago.

"Well, I'm glad someone is awake at this moment," another voice boomed.

Stin scoffed. He didn't need to see a doctor—he needed to soothe the alter ego inside him desperately trying to get out. Icicles started to form in his blood, creating a stabbing pain that escalated throughout his entire body. If he didn't get out of here soon, he was going to explode. "How are you—"

Stin held his hands up, cutting her off. "If one more person asks me how I'm doing, I'm gonna scream. It's bad enough my alter ego feels like I'm about to explode."

Stin watched Ford scratch his head. At that moment, Gabriel Sanchez, another member of the Truson S.E.T., had walked in to catch up on all the festivities.

If Gabriel and Ford knew about the attack, then surely Tonia did too. He stiffened. Where was she?

Stop doing this to yourself. You were the one that stated you didn't want to be anywhere near her.

Stin couldn't help but shake the dark and horrible shadow he envisioned in his brain. Something wasn't right, and he needed to figure it out fast before anyone got hurt. Stin heard the doctor say something about checking his vitals, but that was the last thing he wanted to hear at the moment.

"Now that you're awake, we can talk about what our next strategy is going to be when it comes to this particular situation. Do you remember the guy who attacked you?"

"I do," Lex said. "I didn't get an opportunity to see his face because of his outfit, but during the mist of the fight, I noticed a small tattoo on his right arm." Lex motioned his finger to his arm. "This is where I saw the tattoo."

“So, you were attacked too?” Stin felt the blood boiling in his chest. His powers were quickly building and his alter ego wanted to scream. No one attacked the people he cared about and got away with it.

“It’s not a big deal,” Lex said, shrugging. “I was able to fight him off with my awesome abilities. You should have seen me.” Lex raised his arms. “I kicked some serious ass.”

“Language,” Ford replied.

Stin had to admit he was proud of his adoptive son for showing off his strength and abilities, but it still didn’t settle the uneasiness he felt about facing his attacker alone. He also couldn’t erase the suspicious feeling that something was definitely wrong when it came to Tonia. He knew he should have stopped caring about her and move on with whatever came his way. He was sure to find plenty of lawyers willing to represent him.

Not like Tonia.

“Son of a bitch.” He needed to find out who his attacker was before he struck someone else. Surely, there was a plan in place to find out whoever was responsible for this—something he was familiar with because of his strong bond with his best friend and boss, Ford. There was no way they were going to get away with it.

“So, what's the plan?” If there was a plan in place, he needed to know what his part would entail. Thoughts of Tonia invaded his head. A part of him didn't want her in this. If he suspected this was the work of the Hammerhead Squad, then she needed to stay away because of their past history of murders and schemes that Stin had known about for years.

Maybe it was a good idea to let her go then, huh?

Ford turned and motioned toward Lex. Stin knew what it meant, but he hoped Lex wouldn’t pick up on it.

Whatever plan they were going to come up with, Lex couldn't be involved. Although Lex stared at Ford, there seemed to be no indication of him stating anything about the gesture. Lex didn't move or say a word to Ford as Ford focused his attention back to Stin.

"Well, one of the plans I've considered deals with you and Tonia. Is she going to represent you in court when it comes to this trial?" Ford stuck his hands in his pockets and stared at him, waiting for his response.

"I hope not. After what she did to me and my friends, I want her to stay as far away from us as possible," Lex piped in then paused. "Wait a minute, what trial? What's he talking about?"

"Lex, I think it's time for you to get ready for school tomorrow. I don't want you to miss anything." Lex folded his arms.

"No, I think I should stick around. I have a feeling you're hiding something from me, and I want to know what it is," Lex said. "So spill, *Daddy.*"

Stin grunted. The term "daddy" was something he didn't want Lex to use since he knew who his father was. Despite the terrible things his father had done to him and his mother, Stin didn't like the idea of him being replaced for his dad. He didn't want Lex to forget who he was or where he came from. He could tell from how he said the word 'daddy' that Lex was going to put up one hell of a fight if he continued to pressure him to leave. Ford turned to Lex.

"I think the discussion should be kept between you and Stin when it comes to the trial. But what I'm about to propose is something that involves both of you due to safety reasons." Ford exhaled. "Since we are not sure who attacked you and Lex, I'm afraid your house might be affected because of this incident."

"Meaning?" Stin said, rolling his hand in the air. "C'mon Ford, get on with it. What are you trying to tell me here?"

"You might have to stay with Tonia until we get all of this sorted out."

"No way!" All eyes were on Lex as he shook his head. "There's no way I'm going to move in with her. I can't even understand how she is a part of this team after everything she's done to me and my friends."

"Lex, I get that you and your friends suffered some major damage due to her feelings toward me, but right now, your safety is at risk, and I can't afford to losc another member of this team." Ford paused.

Stin saw how emotional he was getting. Hell, he couldn't even handle his emotions right now.

Time to change the subject.

"Maybe we should talk about this later. Hey, I know!" Stin sat up on the bed and raised his hand. "Who wants to go surfing?" That should have made the situation a little more bearable, at least on his part anyway. Now wasn't the time to let emotions take over—not when there were enemies out there who were trying to kill them because of a crime he didn't commit.

Story of my life.

Ford shifted his weight as Stin's alter ego continued scratching at the surface. He couldn't take it much longer. He tried to fight it off as much as he could, but the human side to him was breaking down. It had been a while since his alter ego had anything to eat or drink. The food at the hospital sucked. As much as he hated to see any sense of anger or sadness between his adoptive son and his best friend and current boss, he needed Ford to tell him what the path was going to be *before* he transformed for the night.

And maybe search for Tonia in the midst of the chaos.

Stin wanted to push past the emotions he felt in his gut, but he couldn't. Despite what he was going through, he still needed to see her, and the only way it was going to be possible was if he agreed to the deal of her representing him in court. Stin nodded.

"Ford, I'm taking you up on the deal. We'll stay with Tonia."

***

Gio strutted toward Blake's wife Jessica Hammerhead as Jessica's head was buried in a line of papers scattered around the desk. Gio stopped just inches away from her before she managed to look up and stop whatever she was doing at the moment. Gio could feel the moisture of heat creeping at his neck, his eyes roaming up and down Jessica's body as she stood up and took a couple of steps toward him.

"Is it done?" were the first words that came out of her mouth. He shouldn't have been surprised she didn't ask how he was feeling throughout the process, but Gio was still hoping one day Jessica would actually care about him enough to have a real conversation with him and not have it be all business all the time.

"Yes, Ms. Hammerhead. Stin got the message and so did his protégé Lex."

Her eyes went wide. "Lex? Isn't that…"

"… Stin's adoptive son. He was there when the attack occurred. The bodyguard tried to fight him off, but he was too strong."

"Did he see who attacked him?" she asked. A wave of panic flew through her. Heat rose in Gio's cheeks. It was unfair that Jessica had to be served this news from him of all people considering her husband Blake had convinced her to plan the attack in the first place. Why was he doing all of this?

"No," Gio responded. He gently pressed his hands-on Jessica's shoulders.

Jessica exhaled and held her chest. "How is Stin?"

"He's fine. But I think that—"

"—I know, I know. We should back off until the trial is over." Jessica buried her face in her hands and sat down. Gio watched as she put her hands down on her legs, rubbing them back and forth. "I just hate what that son of a bitch did to my Jojo." With one hand over her mouth, Jessica let out a low sob.

I can't stand to see her hurting like this...

Gio wrapped his hands around her shoulder and laid her head down. He knew the tears were there, but he couldn't feel the moisture through his dark blue tuxedo vest. Not that he minded Jessica crying on his shoulder, but the suit was costly, which meant another trip to the cleaners to get it washed.

In his eyes, the trip was worth it if it made Jessica's pain and sadness go away even if it was just for a little while.

A shallow noise escalated from the room, causing both of them to turn their heads. Gio grunted when he saw Blake Hammerhead staring at both of them, his eyes focusing more on Jessica than him. The question of Blake's whereabouts charged through Gio's mind as Blake inched closer to them.

Don't touch her. You don't deserve her.

"Oh Blake!" Jessica quickly moved out of Gio's embrace and ran into the arms of her husband. Envy sliced at Gio's heart. If only she could see who Jessica was dealing with when it came to a man like Blake Hammerhead…

"What happened my love? Why the tears?" Blake asked, interrupting Gio's thoughts.

"I just want Stin to pay for what he did. It seems like no matter what I do, he's always getting away with something. He can walk around and have this normal, happy life while my daughter is suffocating somewhere in the damn ocean!" Jessica slammed her fists in mid-air. Blake rubbed her shoulders before he decided to bury Jessica's face in his hands.

"I promise you, once Stin goes to trial and the jury finds him guilty, everything will be over."

"But what if it's not? What if—" Gio watched as Blake placed one finger over her lips. The gesture was enough to make him puke.

"Jessica, relax. Stin won't be found innocent of anything." He paused. "I have all the proof I need to send Stin away for a really long time, but you're going to have to be patient with me and trust what I am telling you, okay?"

Yeah, that you are a scum bag who likes to lie and keep secrets from your wife?

Gio squeezed his hands tighter as he watched Blake give a final kiss on the forehead before ushering Jessica to go take a walk.

"I want him dead, Blake. I want him dead."

"I know and it's going to happen, but you have to be patient," Blake said. "I have some business to take care of with Gio. I think you should go for a walk."

Jessica nodded but didn't say another word as she made her way out the door and into the warm sun that bombarded the entire island for the duration of the summer. As Gio watched the reflection of the sun cascading off the aquamarine ocean stationed outside the Hammerhead Headquarters, his mind couldn't help but wonder how long it was going to be before everything crashed into pieces.

"What are you thinking about? Why are you so quiet, Gio?"

Blake's voice echoed through his thoughts. Gio closed his eyes as his other side protested at his boss. He thought about controlling his anger before he turned to face the one man he despised so severely it took everything he had not to grab his gun and shoot him.

Then you would have to explain it to Jessica.

"Don't you hear me talking to you?" Blake asked again.

"I was just wondering when you are going to tell your wife the truth," Gio said. Gio stepped closer to his boss. "Don't you think your wife deserves to know the truth?" Gio watched his boss as he poured a glass of vodka and took a swig.

"Do you think I like lying to my wife about these things? I feel terrible about lying to her like this."

Gio scoffed.

"Do you feel terrible about what you've done to Jojo? How about what you did to her unborn child?"

Blake stiffened.

Gio knew he'd hit a nerve when it came to this situation. He hated lying to Jessica when it came to Jojo. He wanted Blake to realize just how much keeping the truth from his own wife was killing him inside.

A part of him wanted to walk away, but he needed to protect Jessica from this beast she called her husband.

"Don't you ever talk about that situation ever again. Do you understand?" Blake demanded, pointing his finger at Gio's face.

Gio flicked Blake's finger away. "I don't have to bring it up to you, *Blake.* You already know what you've done. But I know Jessica doesn't know what you've done," Gio replied. His jaw clenched. Gio felt his hands balling up when Blake took his third swig of vodka before he made his way to Gio.

"I see you are having a bit of an issue when it comes to keeping your mouth shut, so let me remind you of what might happen if you violate your duties." With swift hands, Blake grabbed Gio's vest and pulled, tugging Gio toward him. The two men were in each other's faces in seconds. Gio felt Blake's warm breath across his face.

"If you so much as spill one word about what happened to anyone, I'll kill you."

Gio wanted to laugh. "Don't you remember Blake? You taught me everything I know. I will slice you to pieces." Silence escalated through both of them. Blake jerked Gio away from him.

Gio straightened his suit with his hands before facing Blake. "What the hell is so funny? You think all of this is a joke, don't you?" Blake grabbed a chair from the other side of the room and flopped down.

"No Gio. I don't think it's a joke." He paused and stared at the huge vodka bottle on the table. "But what I think is funny is that you are going around making threats while forgetting who I am. If you disobey my rules when it comes to this situation, I will remind Jessica and her friends about the horrible treatment you have given me when it comes to your line of service. Once that happens, all I have to do is give her friends the command, and those great teeth of great white sharks will have you killed." The intensity in his eyes said it all. Gio knew that as soon as he said it, he meant every word.

Great whites ripping and tearing into his skin was not his idea of fun. His body would be in pieces in seconds. Before Gio could try another sound, two bodyguards strutted their way inside.

"Is everything okay in here, sir?" one of the bodyguards asked.

"Everything's fine," Gio barked. Gio gave out one final stare at the man who just threatened his life. He turned to the other bodyguards. "Let's go." Gio didn't manage to turn around to see if the other bodyguards followed suit. He couldn't have cared less.

He wanted out of this business.

He shouldn't have to put up with a boss who he knew killed the one person who mattered more to his wife than anyone in this world. Jojo may have done a lot of stupid, crazy things in her life, but Gio knew Jojo was going places. She didn't want to be a part of the Hammerhead Headquarters like Jessica wanted. She had her own path to follow.

Until Blake ruined it by expressing his sexual desires.

Gio didn't know how much longer he could take hiding the truth from Jessica. As far as he was concerned, this had gone far enough, and he wasn't going to continue with these lies his boss told everyone. It was at that moment he made a decision, one in which put his entire future at stake.

A task he didn't mind losing…

***

How could she possibly explain her case to Stin about representing him?

That was the question looming through Tonia's mind as she tried to make herself comfortable in her bedroom. She tapped the pen on a bright yellow legal pad begging for her attention. She couldn't understand why she wanted to represent him in the first place, considering his behavior the other night. Dismissing her after their one-night stand should have sent alarms ringing through her mind.

But this would look good for you. You would be able to get more clients and maybe...

"...start my own law firm?" Tonia said out loud. Tonia reflected on her comment. For years she had been an independent agent working with clients on her own to win cases, but this was the first time she was going to represent someone guilty of murdering a sixteen-year-old girl. If she won, there was a huge possibility she could get the publicity she needed to run her own law firm. The more Tonia thought about it, the more excited she got.

There was no way Stin would be able to deny her this offer. She finally had something to fight for, and she wasn't going to back down anytime soon.

Her cellphone buzzed just as she was about to write the opening statement. She glanced at the number and grunted before she decided to answer.

"Hello, Mr. Mayfield, how are you this evening?"

"Fine," he replied. The tone in his voice was different. Confusion probably etched in his brain because of the formal greeting Tonia gave out. In the past, Tonia always referred to him by his first name, but since he declared his love to Mandy Stevenson, the situation changed. She needed to distance herself from it as much as possible, and the only way she was going to be able to do it was if she started treating him like a boss.

"Uh, I'm sorry for calling you. I know you're very busy, but I need to ask you for another favor..."

"Mr. Mayfield—"

"Ford, Tonia. It's Ford."

"Not anymore," she barked unexpectedly. She gained her composure as she started the conversation again. "I've already expressed to you that Stin doesn't want my—"

"—I already heard what you said, Tonia. There is no need to repeat it. As much as you have stated Stin's disapproval of this entire situation, I'm afraid Stin isn't thinking about what's best for him at the moment, which is why I am calling you."

Tonia let the comment sink in. She wasn't sure what Ford was getting at, but Tonia had a feeling she didn't want any part of it.

"What is this about Mr. Mayfield?"

"Due to the recent attack on Stin and Lex, I think it would be best if Lex and Stin stayed at your cabin until all of this is over."

"Why?" she asked. "Stin is more than capable of taking care of himself. I know he got attacked unexpectedly, but Stin's powers are pretty strong. He can handle himself quite well." Tonia recalled some incidences where Stin had to use his powers to destroy enemies who threatened to take down the Truson Super Elite Team.

"That may be so Tonia, but considering the unknown number of Hammerheads who are ready to destroy him because of Jojo's death, I can't risk Lex and Stin sleeping in the cabin. I think it would just be safer if they stayed with you until all of this is over," he said.

"And if I disagree with this decision?" The thought of Stin being so close to her rattled her in a way she didn't expect. Visions of their one-night stand flooded through her mind. She could feel the heat in her cheeks rising while the images of him touching her in the most intimate ways flashed in front of her.

"Tonia, this is an order. I'm afraid you have no choice in the matter. Stin is in a lot of trouble, and it's up to us to help him through this. I know you can't stand to be around each other, but you two have to suck it up until Stin is found innocent of all these charges, and the Truson S.E.T. finally gets revenge."

Tonia exhaled and mulled over everything her boss said. "Ford?"

"Yes?"

"I hate it when you're right."

CHAPTER FIVE

It tore at his skin again and again, each one more painful than the last. Stin tried to remember the last time his alter ego was ever this aggressive. He wanted to explode. The ice forming inside his veins felt like swords tearing away at his body.

"So, wait a minute—what happened again?"

Stin turned his attention to Gabriel, who was now catching up to the latest incident involving his recent attack.

"Stin was attacked using some sort of liquid that caused him to bruise and lose unconsciousness," Ford said.

"Do we know what kind of powder it is?" Gabriel asked, shifting his glances between Stin and Ford.

"I'm not exactly sure what it is, but I do know it's some sort of substance the Hammerheads used a long time ago to kill their enemies." Ford paused. "Stin's lucky to be alive."

Stin continued to squirm in his bed but pretended the level of discomfort he was facing didn't bother him by smiling and nodding his head at Ford's suggestion. Besides the fact his alter ego roared louder than the ocean outside the window, he couldn't stop thinking about Tonia. The vivid dreams of her being attacked caused him to lie awake half of the night. He had only slept for two hours because of his thoughts of Tonia and his one-night stand with her.

"Isn't there going to be some sort of retaliation for

this? I mean, our friend got hurt here, shouldn't we be arranging some sort of plan to retaliate?" Gabriel asked.

"Believe me, I thought of that idea, but due to the pending murder case looming over Stin's head, I'm afraid that's going to have to wait."

"Murder charge? What murder charge?" Silence filled the room as Stin gripped the silver lining across his bed. He took a couple of deep breaths as Ford raised a brow. Stin took it as a sign he was allowed to state his side of the story.

"I was recently charged with killing a sixteen-year-old girl name Jojo Hammerhead," Stin said.

"How? Why are they accusing you of this?"

"The Hammerheads are claiming a witness saw an orca attacking Jojo and leaving her to die in the ocean. The witness stated the orca had a blue marking on its belly—"

"—meaning that Stin did it," Gabriel finished.

Another wave of pain coursed through Stin, this time landing in his chest. Another round of deep breaths escaped his lungs.

"Where was Stin?"

"Surfing the waves," Stin said in a rush. "Jojo always had a crush on me. I wanted to nail a chick in bed but she ruined it for me." Those were the last words Stin could muster before he scooted and scurried out the door.

Need water! Need Water! Need Water!

The words repeated in his brain over and over again until he managed to open the doors to the outside air. The sun had disappeared behind the low clouds forming over the ocean. The air smelled of dirt mixed with ocean water as Stin darted toward the sea, unafraid of what was about to happen.

"Stin! Stin, Where—"

Before he could hear Ford ask his question on his whereabouts, Stin dived headfirst into the ocean. The water welcomed his muscles as they began to tighten and stretch across his body. It only took a matter of seconds for him to form into his alter ego.

He had been grateful for that at least.

The smell of food was everywhere. Stin relaxed. He studied the fish swimming around in circles. His stomach growled at the sight as he wasted little time moving in for the kill. Salmon happened to be his favorite meal of the day, and the more he ate it, the more his body began to enjoy this little adventure he needed after spending time cooped up in his hospital bed.

How long had it been since he was in that bed? His body felt like he was in a coma for a month. His fin was aching, but his flippers made it easy to swim at a steady pace. Stin tried to remain focused on the task at hand, but he had to admit it was very challenging.

Especially when something else had distracted him from his early morning meal.

Stin bit down on the latest salmon that didn't stand a chance against him when he spotted another killer whale swimming away. Stin let the salmon swim away and remained focused on the killer whale. He swam closer, hoping to get a better look at what was happening. He immediately sprung to action when he saw the Hammerhead open up his mouth and bite down on the orca's flipper. The surprise came when the orca he was trying to save ended up splashing a green liquid upon the hammerhead's face.

Tonia!

He was the only one who knew what her powers were truly capable of. He had experienced it himself when they got into an argument when she decided to follow Ford around like a lovesick puppy. Whoever the great hammerhead was that decided to tackle her was in for a rude awakening. Stin swam faster as the hammerhead swam back and started swinging his head. Stin watched the poison go through the hammerhead's veins and then his bones before his body exploded into pieces. Before he was able to reach Tonia, a second hammerhead snuck up beside her.

There's no way you're going to hurt her. I'll kill you.

Stin swam up and barreled his teeth on the side of the hammerhead, breaking the connection between Tonia and him. Somehow, Stin felt the panic bubbling inside her as her powers shot out during the battle before she managed to focus and crash into the assailant. He felt the impact, sending him spiraling as a wave of water boiled underneath them. It was obviously a clear invitation that Tonia wanted to continue the battle above the water.

Which suited Stin well. As a matter of fact, he was tired of the whole underwater scene. If he was going to fight to protect Tonia, he was going to do whatever it took to keep her safe.

Stin felt the blast of water course through him as he lifted his entire body out of the water in mid-air, spinning until he made a hard thud onto the sand. Stin coughed. The sand elevated him in a storm. It wasn't until the sand finally disappeared into the hostile sun that he realized what was happening right in front of him.

The man who had been the unknown Hammerhead he had attacked earlier was now grabbing Tonia by her legs and pushing himself on top of her. Stin got to his feet as Tonia used her powers again to fight off the attacker.

Get your filthy hands off of me. As Tonia's thoughts ran through Stin's brain, he was grateful Tonia was defending herself so well. Before the attacker could recover from his wounds, Stin grabbed him and sent his fist flying into the attacker's face, knocking him off his feet.

"Stin?" Tonia's voice rang out. All eyes were focused on the attacker as his jaw turned into ice. Stin stood a couple of inches back and watched the unknown assailant turn into a popsicle before he focused his attention on Tonia.

"Are you all right?" he asked.

"Stin, what the hell were you thinking? Why would you do something like this?"

"Excuse me?" Stin felt the tension in his jaw and saw the flash of anger in Tonia's eyes before she spoke again.

"I could have handled that guy myself. I didn't need you to come swooping in to rescue me like a lovesick puppy. Who do you think I am?"

"A woman that needed help," he stated. "Obviously, you needed my help. You were struggling with your powers." Tonia squinted, and Stin couldn't understand why it was so hard for this woman to accept help when it was needed.

"I wasn't struggling with anything," she said. She leaned forward, her eyes intense on his face. "I was doing just fine on my own."

"That's not what it looked like to me. It seemed to me like you were trying to gain control of the situation but you were losing." There, he'd said it. He didn't want to admit what he saw right in front of his eyes, but he wasn't going to apologize for what he had done. No one was allowed to touch her in his presence except him.

That thought both surprised and excited him.

Silence escalated through both of them before Tonia lifted her hand and caressed his face.

"Your face is healing."

"You still didn't answer my question." More silence. Stin wanted to read her thoughts, to know what she was thinking at the moment but he couldn't. The only time they were able to read thoughts was when they were underwater. The massage of her hands cradling against his face sent an unwavering sensation throughout his entire body.

His abdomen awakened and responded to her touch like the ice spreading through her veins. Tonia's hand slid down his face before he grabbed it with his other hand. He leaned in closer.

"I'm fine."

"I'm glad. So am I," he replied. He expected her to say some remark about him being too close. She shifted her weight.

"I have to go," she said.

"Not right now," Stin said before he pressed his lips against hers.

***

Stop him! Her brain screamed. Her mind tried to replay everything that had happened since that one-night stand. Her mind became a blur, Stin's tongue gently made its way into her mouth, both of them eventually finding a rhythm that neither one could escape. She buried his face in her hands, the kiss getting deeper every second. She felt the moisture growing in-between her legs.

"Stin?"

The voice stopped her. She jerked her head and tried to regain her composure. Tonia saw the dazed expression on Stin's face before he gazed at her. She managed to catch her breath and became grateful for the interruption.

"Lex, what are you doing out here?" Stin asked.

Tonia shifted and focused on the conversation at hand.

Lex shrugged.

"Funny. I wanted to ask you the same thing considering you're supposed to be in the hospital." Lex stuck his hands in his pockets and remained silent.

"I'm fine," Stin finally said. "My face is healing." He paused. "I think you should ask Tonia how she's doing at the moment." Lex raised a brow. Tension rose in the air.

Tonia didn't want to be the one that caused any type of conflict between them. She knew deep down she could apologize for what she had done to Lex and his friends, but Tonia knew there was always that possibility Lex would hate her for the rest of his life and there was nothing she could do to make up for it.

And a relationship with Stin would make it so much worse...

"I'm fine," she muttered. Her heart drummed in her chest. Her legs felt a little weak, but she knew she had to relay the message and try to get as far away from both of them as possible. She kept her focus on Lex as the conversation between her and Ford echoed in her brain. "I just came out here for a swim. No big deal."

"Unfortunately, it was. You could have gotten yourself killed if I wasn't there," Stin replied.

She wanted to argue with him about what he really saw when they were in the ocean but decided to drop it.

"By the way, how did you end up being attacked in the first place?"

"Stin, are we heading back to the cabin? There's something I need to show you. It's something I think you'll like," Lex said.

Tonia hoped Stin would drop the subject and try to spend time with Lex so she could take her mind off what just happened. That kiss left her wanting more than she ever could imagine.

Something she knew she shouldn't have any part of.

Instead, Stin's baby blue eyes were locked with hers.

Tension and passion all rolled into one when Stin opened his mouth and told Lex to meet him back at the cabin. She then remembered what she needed to say before the hammerheads managed to ensue chaos on her peaceful day.

"Lex can't go back to the cabin and neither can you," she announced. "Ford's orders."

Stin shrugged.

"Good because I wasn't planning on staying at my cabin tonight."

"What do you mean?" Lex said. "Where else are we gonna stay besides our cabin?"

Tonia's alter ego stirred within her. *They have to stay with you.* Those were the arrangements Ford had put in place. She had to do her job to protect the team. Nothing else.

You sure about that? She ignored the last statement and let it out.

"Ford has issued orders that both of you to stay with me until the trial is over."

"Meaning he had suspicions about the Hammerheads coming after you?"

"Meaning he was worried about your safety," Tonia argued.

"I'm not staying in that cabin with her. Not after what she did to me." Lex strutted past Tonia and was inches from Stin. Tonia held her breath and waited for Lex to lose control so she could try her best to control the situation without anyone getting hurt.

"Please tell me you are not considering this."

"I'll leave you two alone." Tonia took a few steps toward the direction of the cabin when she felt someone grab her arm.

"Tonia, wait."

She closed her eyes. Heat surged through her as Stin's fingers grasped her wrists. Despite the impact his touch had on her, she still managed to keep her back to him.

"Stin, we can talk about this later. I think it's more important you work it out with Lex." There. She hoped that would break whatever contact they had with each other so she would be able to focus on what she needed to do to get through the day. Being in constant contact with Stin Vanderson had made her confused and excited all at the same time.

The last thing she needed was to spend another night with the man who dumped her like yesterday's garbage. Knowing Stin's history with women, he loved the one-night stands without the commitment. Stin Vanderson was a playboy at heart, and Tonia didn't want any part of it. She'd already experienced that once in her life, and she didn't want to go back to that again.

"Stin? Are we going back to the cabin or what?" Tonia moved away from Stin and continued walking in the opposite direction.

"Lex, meet me back at the cabin. Start packing your things."

"This blows. There's no way I'm moving in with her."

Tonia turned and glanced as Lex went in the other direction. "Aren't you going to stop him?" she demanded, her accent sweeping between her words. "Something could happen to him, Stin. You can't risk his safety."

Stin nodded. "You're right, I can't," he said.

With one swipe, Tonia felt his hand grip her arm again, this time a little more forcefully than she expected. "Stin, what do you think you're doing?"

Stin ignored her response as he called Lex's name. Lex continued to walk in the opposite direction, ignoring his calls.

"Stin, he doesn't want to come with us—"

"He has no choice in the matter. I'm his legal guardian, he has to do what I say," Stin barked. Tonia could tell he was losing the argument between himself and Lex. To make matters worse, she was about to lose the argument with Stin as well. She felt the intensity of her emotions through her veins, giving her a clear warning that if she didn't break contact with Stin, she was going to repeat the same pattern she did whenever her anger got the best of her.

How in the hell was this arrangement going to work if she couldn't even control herself around him?

"Don't you think it would be wiser if you backed off a little?" She paused, waiting for him to do or say something that would cause her to strike at him like the way it used to be before. But when he focused on her, the cold glint in his eyes was an indication she'd hit a nerve.

"Don't you think it would be wise if you did the same thing?"

The poison in her veins was boiling. She needed to move away from him. She tried to wiggle out of his grasp, but he held firm. Her eyes lifted to his. The intensity she felt between them was too much for her to handle.

"Stin, let me go." Tonia saw his throat move while he swallowed.

"I can't, not after what happened today," he said.

Tonia repeated the words over again in her mind. She couldn't help but wonder if there was more to this relationship than he was letting on? "Stin-"

"How did it happen, Tonia? How did you get attacked in the first place? What happened?"

Silence.

There was no reason for him to know more about anything than what he knew now. If there were ever a time where she needed to set boundaries in terms of how this arrangement was going to work, now would be it.

"Stin, it's none of your business. I need you to stop worrying about me and focus on Lex before he becomes another target. Even though we are going to be living together, we are just going to be partners in a murder trial—that's it. From this very moment, you cannot ask me about my life, and I cannot ask you about yours."

Stin's eyebrows lifted, and Tonia saw a flash of his eyes. He exhaled.

"If that's the way you want it," he said through gritted teeth. He closed his eyes and exhaled. He nodded before he took a couple of steps back and turned in the other direction, heading toward Lex.

"Stin?" Tonia waited for him to turn around again, but it never happened. She called out his name but there was no response. Tonia watched Stin catch up to Lex before they disappeared. She should have been grateful Stin had finally listened to her and focused on Lex after the danger he faced when it came to the Hammerhead squad. So why did she feel so guilty about what just happened?

Well, she wasn't going to just stand there and let the guilt invade her brain. After all, it was his fault. *He* was the one who took advantage of the situation when she decided to be left alone that night. She wasn't the one trying to take advantage, all she wanted was to wallow in her heartache about losing the one man who she thought understood her like no one else. Now she was here, trying her best to reason with her one-night stand when all he did was tell her what a great night he had and that he never wanted to see her again.

He was about to get his wish.

Tonia walked back to her cabin. Amid her strutting, she picked up the phone and dialed Ford's number. After the third ring, a very familiar voice responded.

"Hello?"

"May I please speak to Ford?"

"Sure, may I ask who's calling?" Mandy asked.

None of your business! Tonia cleared her throat and continued the conversation by giving her name.

"Is something wrong, Tonia? Maybe I can help you..."

"No, that's okay Mandy. I just want to speak to my boss please."

"Okay, hold on a sec," she said.

Tonia didn't know she was holding her breath until she felt the air rush out of her lungs when Ford answered the phone.

"Truson S.E.T., this is Ford Mayfield speaking—"

"—I can't do this Ford," Tonia said, cutting him off. At this point, a formal introduction was unnecessary. She needed to get out of this deal. "I thought I could, but I don't think Stin and I will get along."

"Tonia, we talked about this. Stin can't go back to his cabin. They will eventually find him and kill him without hesitation," he said, reminding her why she needed to do it. "Stin and Lex need a place to stay and considering you're his only hope in freeing him, they'll be a lot safer with you."

"But what about Su-Lee and Gabriel? Hell, you're his best friend, why can't he live with you?" she barked. "Why is it that I have to be the one to protect him?" She didn't want the repercussions of what could happen if they got too close to each other again. There was a long pause between them as Tonia waited on his response. Clearly, he could hear the annoyance in her voice. She knew she had agreed to the deal to do what was best for the team, but after today, that no longer seemed possible.

"Tonia, I don't know what happened between you and Stin, and frankly, I could care less about how you two feel about each other—"

"—But—"

"—But you will do what I'm asking you to do. Need I remind you that you agreed to protect Lex and Stin by any means necessary?"

"And if I don't?" she challenged. Her mind screamed to take back the comment, but she ignored it. Her alter ego stirred in a way that made her feel incredibly nervous.

"Then I will have no choice but to suspend you from your duties as a member of the Truson Super Elite Team." Another pause. "Are you sure you want to risk that?"

Tonia couldn't believe what she was hearing. Her being kicked out as a member of the Truson S.E.T.? How dare he threaten such a thing? Ford knew about the hell she had gone through before Dr. Courtney Madison, a brilliant pharmacologist who mixed dead human and animal cells to bring humans back to life as Ormans, came into her life and transformed her into a brand new woman—a woman capable of making her own choices and fighting her own battles instead of the defenseless, puny child that became a victim of violence and abuse back in Africa.

"Ford, don't do this."

"You leave me with no choice Tonia. I'm sorry, but we all have to do our part to stick together through all of this, and it includes you as well. I gave you an assignment, follow through on it."

Tonia opened her mouth to protest but was interrupted by the dial tone buzzing in her ear. She removed the phone from her eardrums and disconnected the call.

So much for trying to get out of the situation…

***

Lex picked up speed as he paced the ground, his shoes crunching against the bright green grass that had invaded the island since the summer began. This was supposed to be the one summer where he wanted to spend time with his new caretaker, Stin. After what his father, Vernon, did by torturing everyone based on his deep love for a woman who was married to someone else, Lex always thought Stin understood what he was going through. Even though Stin became his legal guardian after Lex was sworn in as a member of the Truson S.E.T. team, Lex felt they were more like buddies than the father and son role they were supposed to play.

Now that was changing.

"Lex, stop!" Stin said, trying to catch up to him. "Lex, we have to talk about this. Running away won't solve anything." Lex kept walking. The last thing he needed to hear was Stin offering him advice on anything. He couldn't believe Stin was considering staying with

Tonia of all people, knowing what happened to him and his friends.

"Just leave me alone," Lex said. "I can't believe you're agreed to live with her after everything she's done to me and my friends."

Lex was surprised when Stin grabbed him by the shoulder and shoved him around, facing him.

"Listen to me. I know how you feel about Tonia, okay? I didn't like what she did to you either. I would love to stay in our nice, cozy cabin, but for right now, it's not safe." He inched closer. "I need you to trust me."

"Trust you?" Lex tensed. He tried to come up with a reason not to trust Stin's judgment. He could have thought up thousands of reasons for not trusting his own father, but Stin had proved to be a different story.

"Why?"

"Because she might be the only person that can help us out of this situation."

CHAPTER SIX

"How bad is it?" Lex asked. Lex tried to control his emotions boiling inside him. He fought his alter ego from coming to the surface by trying to hold what he was feeling inside. Lex saw Stin's jaw tense up when he asked the question, giving into Lex's worst fears.

"I've been accused of killing someone, and the only one who can help me out of it is Tonia." Stin paused.

"Stin, there are other lawyers out there willing to represent you—"

"Not like Tonia." Stin rammed his fingers through his hair.

"Lex, no one from the outside world is supposed to know who we are. If everyone knew we were Ormans, they would kill us. This isn't just some ordinary murder son, they're claiming I killed someone from the Hammerhead Squad. What lawyer do you know who would represent someone like that?"

Lex thought about his question. Although he never sat down and read the Book of Truson, he was aware of the consequences when it came to the rules being broken once someone was sworn in as a member of the Truson S.E.T. All Lex could do was nod his head.

"You mean to tell me Tonia is the only one who can help you out of this?" Lex knew the answer to that question. A part of him wanted to say otherwise, based on their history of what he and Tonia had gone through.

"Yes. Tonia is the only one who can help me out of this. Once she does, and we find out who the real killer is, everything will be back to normal."

Lex scoffed.

"How can you say that? She may be representing you in court, but what happens after the trial is over?" *Are you going to sleep with her?* was the question that loomed in his brain. What if they formed some type of relationship while they worked to set Stin free? His alter ego felt like bursting out of his skin. He couldn't deal with this conversation anymore. He had to leave.

"Then everything will go back to the way it was before. We will be living together, and Tonia will continue to do what she loves to do."

Lex wanted to believe that, but after seeing what happened between them, he thought otherwise.

"I gotta go," Lex said, ending the meaningless conversation. "I'm just going to hang out with my friends for a while."

Stin nodded. "I know you have to think about a lot of things, and it's okay. Just try to come back before it gets too dangerous outside."

Lex nodded and then picked up the pace. He needed to be in an isolated area, one in which no one would be able to see him transform into his alter ego. After running for what seemed like hours, Lex finally found a spot behind a couple of trees, blocking off the view from the rest of the island.

The strength of his body quickly landed him on the ground, the rocks ripping and stretching his skin like a rubber band until the rocks and stones were able to pierce his skin and show its true form. Once he knew the transformation was complete, Lex ran farther into the trees to find his friends. He knew he had a million things he needed to do to prepare for school, but for right now, he just wanted to get away from the drama interfering in his life. He needed to see his friends and maybe do the one thing he knew would distract him from everything he didn't want to think about for the next hour…

Surfing.

***

As much as Stin wanted to say no to his decision, he couldn't. What was the matter with him? The Hammerheads were after every person he cared about, including Lex. If anything, he should have demanded Lex stayed with Tonia until the danger was over. He was already attacked once, who was to say the Hammerheads weren't going to attack him again? At the same time, Stin remembered the horrible time Lex had when it came to his own father trying to control Lex's every move.

A part of him didn't want Lex to think he was anything like his father. But as his legal guardian, wasn't it his job to protect Lex at all costs?

As more thoughts centered in his head, Stin walked toward the trees where Lex had gone. He began to second guess his decision once he found out what Lex was doing.

Let him go for now. He will be able to defend himself if necessary. Flashes of the Hammerhead attacking Tonia invaded his thoughts. He wanted to know who the Hammerhead was and how many were trying to go after Tonia. He needed to go back and make sure she was safe. But as Lex's legal guardian, he needed to make sure Lex wasn't being hurt or attacked by them.

There was only one solution to this problem.

Stin got out his phone and dialed Ford's number. After a few rings, Ford picked up.

"Ford?"

"Yeah?"

"Hey man, I'm sorry for disturbing you, but I need you to do me a huge favor."

"Is everything all right?" Ford asked. "There were no other attacks, right?"

"No, nothing like that except for—" His voice trailed off. He didn't want Ford to worry about Tonia's safety. Since they were all going to be roommates until the trial was over, he felt there was no need for Ford to worry about her when he had his own problems.

"—Except for what, Stin? What's going on?"

"I was hoping you could do me a favor and watch over Lex for a while. I'm really worried about him because of what happened the other day. I broke the news to him about moving in with Tonia and about the trial. He doesn't seem happy about the situation."

"Have you tried talking to him? I'm sure he probably feels some resentment about the whole idea, considering how Tonia treated him," Ford said. Flashbacks invaded Stin's mind. Visions of Tonia trying to use her powers to fend off Lex and his friends sent shivers down his spine. He remembered how much he couldn't stand the sight of her every time she came up to him, asking him about Ford or one of the other members of the Truson S.E.T. so that she could relay a message from Dr. Madison about something.

Now? He felt different. After the one-night stand, he wasn't quite sure how he felt. All he knew was he wanted her again—but this time, sober. "I tried, but it doesn't seem like he wants to listen to reason. Unfortunately, something has come up, and I really don't want Lex to be by himself. Could you please send someone to watch him just in case?" Stin asked. He felt guilty for letting Lex go, but he had to get to Tonia to figure out who the attacker was so he could prevent it from happening again.

"All right, Stin. I'll go talk to him about living with Tonia. Are you okay? How's your face?"

"My face is doing a lot better than before. As a matter of fact, my face is the last thing I'm worried about."

Dude, don't say anything else. Silence formed between them. He needed to get off the phone before he managed to say anything else he was going to regret later.

"Why? Did something else happen?" was the next question Ford managed to ask.

Anxiety filled his veins as he searched for Tonia, looking for any signs of danger lurking along the shores of the island.

"Stin? Are you there?"

"Yeah, I gotta go. Can you just keep an eye on Lex? He needs it."

"Sure."

Before Ford could say anything, Stin headed back to Tonia's house. As he approached the door to her luxurious cabin, he tried to remember those awful feelings again whenever she was around him. Stin took his fist and pounded on the door. His alter ego stirred, but he managed to control himself as he heard someone fiddle with the lock. It didn't take long for her to reveal herself.

Stin held his breath. The short hair he was used to seeing daily was replaced by long, curly, light-brown hair that flowed to her back. Her eyes seemed lighter and more carefree than what he was used to. His eyes roamed down the long black and white dress that curved her body. His alter ego roared like a lion while his abdomen stirred.

Hate her, remember?

Tonia rolling her eyes brought him back to reality.

“Stin, what do you want? I thought you were going after Lex?”

Stin barged his way into her living room and paused. The room was simple: A TV sat directly across from the door, an all-white couch on the left side of the room with a small cocktail table that was too close to the window. There were no pictures of her home life or anything that represented something about her life before she got involved with the Truson Super Elite Team.

“I need to know what happened today. I need to know how it started,” Stin said, still facing the TV. “The sooner I know what happened, the better.” He heard a sigh come out before he managed to come face-to-face with her.

She crossed her arms.

“I’m afraid that’s none of your business,” she replied. A horrible pain in his chest caught him by surprise. He shook the pain off.

“It is when it comes to the people I care about.” He paused as he inched closer to her. She took a step back.

“Why are you smiling like that?” she asked.

“I’m not smiling.”

“Yes, you are and it’s annoying. I want you to stop.”

Stin saw how annoyed she was getting and couldn’t help but want more. *Hate her, remember?*

The silence was killing him even more. As he stared into her light brown eyes and pink lips, he moaned. His mind replayed the one-night stand again. He became surprised by his reaction. This was only supposed to be a partnership between an attorney and her client who just so happened to be the same woman he slept with.

Be serious dude, someone is after you. You need to know who it is.

"If I stop smiling, will you tell me what happened between you and that asshole? I need to know."

Tonia shrugged her shoulders.

"Why? Why do you need to know that Stin? He wasn't coming after you, he was after me—"

"—And that's the point, Tonia." The reaction on Tonia's face made him realize his voice had gone higher than he wished. "Don't you understand? These people are going after everyone that comes close to me—including you."

"And why do you care? Let's face it. You hate my guts. You can't stand me being in the same room with you."

Stin felt his eyes burn.

"Because I don't want to see you get killed," he said, lowering his tone. Silence invaded the room once again. "Whoever is after you is after Lex too. Do I have to remind you of what happened earlier?" Stin watched her hands shake before he saw the tears forming in her eyes. *What had he done?*

He just wanted the truth about what happened between her and the Hammerhead. He didn't want to become a jerk. He wanted to apologize but decided not to. All he could do was stand back as Tonia cleared her throat and controlled herself.

"What happened today was none of your business. As far as you and I are concerned, we are business partners, that's it," she said. Stin watched as she turned and headed for the stairs.

"Where are you going?" he asked.

She lifted her head before her eyes met his.

"I'm going to write the opening statement for this trial. If you still want me to represent you, I would suggest you follow my orders and leave me alone."

Stin couldn't say anymore as her shadow disappeared from his sight.

***

How could she ever sleep with a man like Stin, Tonia would never know. As she made her way to her bedroom, Tonia had promised herself one thing out of the situation—she was never going to sleep with Stin as long as she lived. If it wasn't for Ford forcing her hand in the matter, she would let him rot in prison or hire someone else that wasn't a member of thc Truson S.E.T. to make his life a living hell.

The thought of him suffering to keep himself from being exposed brought a huge smile to her lips.

But you would be exposed too. She cursed herself for the reminder and sat down in the chair. She grabbed her legal pad and set it down on the table when she heard her cell buzzing in her ear. She looked at the number before she decided to answer.

"Hello Ford, what's up?" she asked, hoping Ford would send her on an assignment that took her mind off of things for a while.

"I don't know. I keep hearing this rumor about an attack on the island, but I was hoping it wasn't true."

Tonia shifted in her seat. The poison coursed through her veins.

"That son of a bitch told you, didn't he?" Tonia balled her fist and slammed it down on the table. "Why can't people learn to mind their own business around here?"

"Uh…who are you talking about Tonia?"

"Do not insult my intelligence, Ford. I'm not stupid. I know who told you this," she replied.

"Really, who?"

"Stin. Am I right?"

"No, you're wrong, but you mentioning Stin gives me the impression he was aware of it as well," Ford said.

Tonia thought about the conversation. Since Stin didn't let his boss and so-called "best friend" know about the attack, Tonia knew there was going to be some consequences.

Good. It's what Stin needs after the way he's treated me.

"So if Stin didn't mention what happened, who did?"

"You should never go out on the island alone unless you alert one of us you're going. You never know what could happen on the—"

"Thank you for the warning, Ford. Can you please answer my question?"

Ford stopped and cleared his throat.

"Tonia, are you—"

"*Ford*, answer the question—please." More silence. It cut her like poison. She felt her powers boiling inside. If Ford didn't tell her who had spied on her, she was going to send poison throughout the entire house.

And maybe paralyze Stin in the process.

"You are not the only one who likes to go out for a swim every once in a while to take your mind off of things. Mandy saw you coming out of the water after you had been attacked. She wanted to help, but she mentioned that another guy who happened to look like Stin came to your rescue. Is there anything you would like to tell me?"

Mandy. The woman who had stolen Ford's heart and was still one of the newest members of the team. Her alter ego stirred.

"That depends. Is Mandy following me now?"

"Do not insult her Tonia, and before you even think of saying anything about her, let me remind you she's not to blame for us not being together."

Tonia wanted to argue that point but decided against it. He would only blame himself for the situation at hand.

"For the record, Mandy wasn't following you—she went out for a swim and happened to see you fighting with someone. Who was it?" The urgency of his voice sent chills down her spine but in a different way. At this rate, he was going to lose just as much control as she had a few minutes ago.

There was no sense in arguing. This could possibly go on for several more minutes, but Tonia didn't have that amount of time, especially now that she knew the trial was going to start within the next couple of days.

"I'm not exactly sure who he was or where he came from, but I know for sure he's a part of the Hammerhead Squad," she said.

"Did he turn?"

"Yes. After I transformed into my human form, The Hammerhead followed me. I saw him transform from a hammerhead back to his human form as well before they started fighting."

"Who?" Ford asked.

Tonia took a breath.

"Stin and the unnamed prick." Ford let out a low sound. More frustration from lack of info.

And they called each other the best of friends?

Tonia huffed.

"So, what happened next?"

"Stin knocked the guy out. He died on impact due to Stin's supernatural strength."

"Was there anyone else around when the incident occurred?"

"Underwater, no. He didn't have a group with him, and it appeared he was acting alone when he changed," Tonia said. Her throat went dry. She needed something to quench her thirst or else she was going to become irritated again. There was a long silence between them, something that left Tonia with thoughts about what happened. Why did Stin rescue her? Since they were on the island, all they did was torment each other. She would even go as far as saying he enjoyed making her miserable.

"You do know what this means?"

"Ford, we can't go into battle right now. It's not a good time for Stin," Tonia reminded him. "Besides, I made it out of the situation without a scratch. Stop worrying about it so much."

"It's not just you I'm worried about Tonia. The Hammerheads are not backing down. They are itching for a fight," he said.

Tonia knew that arguing with him wasn't going to do any good. The best she could do was warn him. Besides, there were more important things in life than dealing with someone as stubborn and bull-headed as Ford.

"If you feel like going to war with the Hammerheads will make you feel better than by all means. Even though you're my boss, I am hereby dismissing myself from any further action between you and the Hammerheads…"

"But—"

Tonia hung up before he could continue the discussion. The last thing she needed was another argument. She had enough of that with Stin. If she still wanted to represent Stin with this murder trial looming over their heads, the first step she needed to take was her opening statement. She couldn't afford any more distractions. She grabbed a pen and a sheet of paper and started writing her statement until she heard a knock at the door. She put her pen down, frustrated at being interrupted once again. She grabbed the knob on the handle and swung the door open.

"If you're looking for another argument, I suggest you look elsewhere," Tonia barked. "I'm busy trying to save your ass for court tomorrow." A huge whiff of shrimps and crabs filled the air as Stin presented the plate to her.

"I thought you might be hungry, so I prepared this for you."

Tonia's taste buds awakened to the sumptuous seafood before her. The presentation looked divine. Tonia tried to remember the last time she had eaten. When her mind drew a blank, she knew she was in trouble.

"I thought maybe we could talk over a nice dinner." A smile crept up on Stin's face as Tonia crossed her arms.

"Really? You want to talk?"

"Yes."

"And what exactly would you like to talk about Stin?" Tonia asked. Before he was allowed to speak, Tonia kept going. "If you say you want information about what happened earlier, then I'm not talking."

Stin shrugged. "I don't—not anymore. I just want to establish some sort of relationship with you considering the circumstances we're in." He ushered the plate in her direction. "Hungry?"

She wasn't buying it. Not in the least.

"Stin, we hate each other, we can't stand to be in the same room together. This is bullshit." Tonia continued to stand in the doorway, causing Stin to come close.

"I know we haven't had the best relationship, but I thought we could at least try…" Stin hung his head.

Tonia knew he was struggling to find the words but wasn't sure if she wanted to save this conversation or not.

Before she could answer, Stin picked up where he'd left off.

"I tried finding other lawyers that deal with Ormans. There are none and considering the rule about our society…"

"…You can't be represented by any human lawyer," Tonia finished. The seafood continued to linger inside her nostrils. Her hands desperately wanted to take a bite of the delicious food, but she knew what it would cost her if she did.

"C'mon Tonia, can we just have a seat and eat a nice dinner together?"

Her stomach and her alter ego seconded the agreement. She knew it was a losing battle. What did it hurt for an attorney and her client to have dinner? A part of her knew it was wrong, but this was the island of Truson. Sometimes the rules had to be broken to serve a greater cause.

The food was her most significant cause.

She stood back and let Stin come in. He smiled before he set the food down on the table. She watched him as he briefly stared at the legal pad that represented what her opening statement looked like: An empty page.

"Working on something, huh?" he asked.

"The opening statement to your murder trial." Tonia sat down in her chair while Stin grabbed another chair from the kitchen and inched closer. Tonia scooted away to keep the distance between them while Stin handed over the plate of seafood to her. Her mouth watered as the shrimp invaded her tongue.

"How's it going with your opening statement? Have any wonderful ideas of how you're going to present your case to the jury?" He forked another shrimp in his mouth.

"Not so well. I keep getting interrupted. By the way, Ford wants an all-out war between us and the Hammerheads."

"I heard."

Tonia stared at him.

"How?"

It took Stin a while before he responded.

"I overheard the conversation between you and Ford. He seemed pretty upset when you told him about that Hammerhead." Tonia buried her face in her hands before stroking her fingers through her hair.

"You were spying on my conversations? What the hell is the matter with you? Don't you have any boundaries when it comes to this arrangement?" Tonia's eyes burned. The poison was rising. She tried to control it by taking some deep breaths, but it was becoming difficult as time passed.

"And you don't seem to realize what I have stated time and time again," he said. He rose from his chair and leaned in close to her. The aura of his scent sent chills down her spine. She couldn't understand this. This was the guy she was supposed to hate with a passion.

"Yeah, and what exactly do I keep forgetting?" she managed her composure despite the close contact. In her mind's eye, Stin Vanderson was stalking her, and there was no way she was going to let him get away with it. "From what I can tell, all you have been doing is stalking me."

"I'm not stalking you, Tonia. The reason why I did what I did was because I wanted to protect you. As long as the Hammerheads are after you and Lex, I'm going to do whatever it takes to protect you whether you like it or not."

Tonia stood up.

"Protection? Since when was I under your protection, huh? You've always hated me and everything I am, and now all of a sudden, you care about my safety and well-being?" Poison sputtered out from her fingers and onto the floor. The sizzle of the gaping hole on the floor between them was enough to get their attention. They stepped back, giving Tonia some breathing room and a chance to calm down. Stin watched the floor before he massaged his neck.

"Look, maybe having dinner was a bad idea," he said, breaking the silence. "I'm just gonna go." Stin moved his way past her and went for the door. "You can keep the meal. Hope you enjoy it."

After that, the door closed, leaving Tonia in silence once again. She stared at the floor and cursed herself for letting her emotions get the best of her. Usually, she was able to control them in petty situations like the one she just experienced. But now? She was losing ground. Lately, everything Stin had done caused her to lose control.

She needed a way out. The promises she'd made to Ford were falling apart. Tonia desperately stared at the plate of seafood on the table before she grabbed her cell and tapped the numbers on her phone. After three rings, a voice answered on the other end of the line.

"Hello?"

"I'm hoping you're not busy Su-Lee because I really need a friend right now."

CHAPTER SEVEN

Thoughts swirled in Stin's brain as he paced back and forth across Tonia's living room floor. He needed air. Fear, anger, despair…he couldn't deal with all of his emotions at once. If it continued to boil, he knew what the end result would be.

Just like Tonia and her powers.

He couldn't understand where all of this was coming from. Any other time he slept with a woman, it only lasted for one night. He never had silly dreams or fantasies about them or wished he could repeat the same process over again. No woman was ever going to make him feel that way.

Or so he'd thought.

No, it can't happen. Stin tried to think of a million reasons why it wouldn't work between them, including the relationship Lex had with her. It was no secret they hated each other, and he could understand why considering how much pain Tonia caused when it came to Lex and his friends.

Yet another reason why they should stay away from each other.

His mind drifted to Lex. He was supposed to be hanging out with his friends while Ford kept an eye on him. Where was he? It was past time for him to come back to the cabin. Stin searched his pocket for his cell and punched in Ford's number. On the second ring, Stin heard a knock at the door. He was relieved when he saw Lex and Ford standing side-by-side in the hallway.

"I was just about to call, I was—"

"Yeah, I know." Ford made his way in with Lex in tow. "I would have brought him sooner, but there was a huge problem."

Stin made eye contact with Lex, not wanting to think about what Lex was up to. Images of his own teenage years skewed his brain.

"What happened out there?" Stin asked.

"Nothing. I don't see why it's such a huge deal anyway. We weren't doing anything wrong."

"I disagree with that theory considering how you could have gotten you and your friends killed," Ford replied.

Stin's jaw clenched. He thought about the different scenarios of what could have happened but decided not to go down that path.

"What exactly did you do Lex? Before you answer, don't even think about lying to me." Lex moved his head to the side and crossed his arms.

"Like I said, it was no big deal. Me and my friends were just having some fun, that's all."

"Oh, so you mean me watching you using your powers to injure innocent people is your definition of fun?" Ford asked. "What would make you possibly think that?"

Lex continued to stare.

"Dude, do you know how much trouble you are in? We can't go around attacking innocent people, Lex. Are you trying to get yourself killed?" Stin waited on his response. Ford cleared his throat to ease the tension, but it didn't work.

"I think I should let you two sort this out. I have to go back to the school anyway." Ford reached for the handle.

"Wait, I need you to stay," Stin said. "I think it's time we discuss some things." Never taking his eyes off of Lex, Stin decided the only way to get this situation under control was to punish him. "Lex, I want you to go to your room—your new room—and don't come out until Ford and I are finished talking."

Lex scoffed.

"There's no way I'm staying here with that freak. I hate her. I can't believe you even agreed to be in the same room with her," Lex said with his hands in the air. "I can live with Teven or Ford, anyone except her."

Stin reached his hand out, causing his powers to fly over the doorknob.

Lex stepped back.

"Perhaps you didn't hear what I said the first time, you're not going anywhere. It's too dangerous for you to be anywhere else. Sleeping over at your friend's house is no longer an option."

Lex shrugged.

"So I can just stay with Ford—"

"Lex, I'm not in the mood for this…"

"May I interrupt?" Ford said. Before anyone was able to say another word, a knock echoed throughout the room. Stin opened up the door.

"Su-Lee, what are you doing here?" Su-Lee inched closer to Stin. The smell of cinnamon and mango burned his nostrils, giving an indication Su-Lee either just gotten out of a shower or put on too much perfume.

"I'm here because of how much of a jerk you're being to my best friend." Su-Lee smacked him straight across the head.

"Su-Lee, you need to be extremely careful when it comes to situations like this. You know how strong our powers are," Ford warned.

Stin double-checked to be sure there weren't any knives or swords freezing into his brain cells.

"Don't worry, I won't be going back to the hospital anytime soon." Stin focused his attention on the bedroom door as Tonia made her way to join the rest of the gang in the living room.

"What is everybody doing in my living room? Can't a woman have at least five minutes alone in her own home?"

"I agree," Su-Lee piped in. Her eyes focused on Stin. "Especially after the stunts you have been pulling lately."

"I don't have time for this. I'm so outta here," Lex said.

"Lex, don't go out of that door—" Stin took a few steps behind him until Ford raised his hand, blocking him.

"Dude, what do you think you're doing?" Stin asked. Ford didn't say anything as he punched the numbers and put the phone to his ear. Stin listened as Ford sent one of the guards to look after Lex and to bring him back to Truson School for Shapeshifters as soon as possible.

"Now, since Lex will be captured and locked up until the wee hours of the morning, I say we leave and let the women get whatever they are feeling off of their chest."

Stin watched Su-Lee squint at the both of them before Ford ushered them out of the door and into the hot blazing sun. *How I miss the winter,* Stin thought. The smell of the seawater hitting against the sand made him feel more alive than anything he could have ever imagined. He thought about the only thing able to calm him down and cursed himself for not thinking about it sooner when it came to him and Lex.

How could he not think about the one thing that had brought him and Lex together in the first place?

"I think it's time for us to take our minds off of what's going on," Ford said, interrupting his thoughts. Once Ford brought out the surfboards, Stin knew precisely what he wanted to do. Stin didn't hesitate to take it when Ford offered.

"What's this, dude? You usually don't surf with me." Stin put the surfboard under his arm. He stared at the people passing by who wanted nothing more than to soak up the sun late in the evening.

"I'm not doing this for me, I'm doing this for you." Ford dusted the little sand left off of the surfboard. "Apparently, you need it from what I can see."

Stin scoffed. He wanted to respond but decided against it.

"So, you want to tell me what's going on or do you want to surf to get all of that extra energy out?"

Stin shrugged and raised his arms in the air.

"What kind of question is that?" He faced the ocean and let the sea breeze flow through his blond curls before he ran to the ocean with his surfboard in tow.

"Race ya to the ocean!" Stin threw the surfboard on the water and landed his feet on the wood. A new set of waves were rising, and he wanted to be the first person to ride them.

***

He didn't want to believe the news.

In one way, his story worked entirely in his favor. Stin killing Jessica's brother John made him even more guilty of murdering Jojo. It was perfect. Stin was going to be found guilty and put away for the rest of his life. He and Jessica were going to live happily ever after.

No more secrets. No more lies. Everything he had built up to this moment was perfect. The only downside was Jessica's broken heart once she found out about Stin's latest attack against another member of her family. She was going to be devastated.

No worries. You will be there to cheer her up.

Blake watched his wife come up from the water and run her fingers through her hair. Tingles went from his stomach to his cock. After all these years, he was surprised the attraction hadn't died and was stronger than ever before. As much as he wanted to take her on the sandy beach, he knew that after he broke the devastating news, the atmosphere was going to change dramatically.

"Are you just going to stand there and watch me swim all day or are you going to join me?" She planted a kiss on his cheek. "Come join me."

Blake stared down at her hands. He debated whether he should tell her at this very moment considering how happy she looked. He moved his fingers across the knuckles of her hands.

"I can't Jessica. I really need to tell you something," he said. He swallowed.

Jessica moved her hands away, but her eyes never moved from his face. The sadness that had plagued her after Jojo's death was still etched in her face. Blake hated himself for even bringing the situation up.

"Did they find Stin guilty yet? Did they find any evidence tying him to Jojo's death?"

Blake cleared his throat.

"Not yet. The trial hasn't started." He paused.

"You know how I feel about that, Blake. I want him dead after what he has done to my daughter. He doesn't deserve to live."

"I know, I know, and you will get your wish, Jessica." He gently replaced a strand of her hair to the back of her ear. "I promise."

Blake watched Jessica fold her arms. "Well, if it's not about getting justice for Jojo then what is there left to talk about? I'm hoping whatever it is it won't…"

"…Your brother John—" He cut her off before he finally managed to speak. "He's dead, Jessica. They found his body this morning."

Her lips quivered. She shook her head.

"No Blake, you're wrong. He's alive, I talked to him two days ago. He's fine," she said.

Blake shook his head, no. He wanted to take the words back, but he couldn't. The fear etched in his wife's face. Tears streamed down her cheeks.

"I'm so sorry baby." Blake reached for her, but she backed away, unable to process what had happened. Her body shook.

"You're wrong, dammit! John's alive and I'm going to prove it." Jessica marched toward her belongings and found her cell.

"Baby, don't do this," Blake pleaded. He tried to grab the phone from her, but she moved back and punched the numbers.

"He's alive. I know he is, and as soon as you hear his voice, you're going to apologize for making me think otherwise." After a few rings, John's voicemail message buzzed her ear. More tears streamed down her face as she hung up and dialed the number once again.

"Jessica, don't do this. He's not going to answer the phone." Blake thought about taking the phone away from her but changed his mind once Jessica threw the phone onto the sand. She buried her face with her hands. Blake wrapped his arms around his wife as she screamed into the sky. Seeing her so depressed about her only brother was enough for him to almost cancel the trial altogether.

Almost.

"How could this happen? Whose responsible for this?" she asked.

"Stin and the Truson S.E.T. arranged the murder. Stin was caught giving John a blow to the jaw. John's face and body was like a frozen popsicle once they found him."

Jessica wiped the last of her tears and grabbed her clothes. Blake put his hand on her arm. "Where are you going? I thought maybe we could go out for a swim…"

"…A swim? Are you joking? I'm going to find that son of a bitch and kill him myself!" Jessica grabbed her jeans from the pile and put them on.

Blake put his hands on her shoulders.

"I know you're stressed out about what happened to John…"

"…Stressed out? My brother is *dead* Blake. I'm more than a little stressed out." Jessica continued mumbling as she finished dressing.

He needed to do something quick. He couldn't let Jessica go out there, seeking revenge on Stin and the rest of his team when everything was going according to plan.

"Listen to me. I know this is going to be very hard for you to understand, but I promise you, Stin and the S.E.T. are going to get what's coming to them. The trial officially starts tomorrow. Within a few weeks, Stin is going to be dead, and no one is going to hurt our family again. Once Stin is gone, then we'll go after the entire team until all of them are dead," Blake said.

"Is everything okay?" a familiar voice said.

Blake grunted. Gio always picked the worst times to pop up.

"I'm going to go lie down." Jessica pushed her way past Gio and headed back to the house, leaving them standing alone.

"So you're up to your old tricks again, huh? What lie did you tell her this time?" Gio asked.

Blake clenched his jaw.

"I didn't lie about anything. Jessica's brother was killed by Stin. Apparently, Stin and John got into it, and Stin killed him with his powers." Gio inched closer. Blake reached his arms out, obviously wanting Gio to congratulate him on his plan.

"I think it's time you tell Jessica the truth, don't you?" Gio asked.

Blake's arms dropped.

"What the hell are you talking about?"

"I don't think Stin should pay the price for something he didn't do."

Blake squinted. Where the hell was this coming from? Thoughts swirled his brain. Out of all the bodyguards he'd hired, Gio used to be his second-in-command. He never used to challenge any of his assignments. Now he wanted to do the right thing?

"Are you working for them now?" Blake barked. "Since when did you start taking their side?"

"Since an innocent man shouldn't have to pay for someone else's crimes. Jessica deserves a husband who's honest with her…not a lying cheating bastard like you."

Blake balled his fists and clenched his teeth. He could feel the Hammerhead coursing through his body. Within seconds, Blake's head turned into his second half, challenged Gio for a fight.

"Well, if you insist." Gio followed Blake's lead. Gio's head transformed, grabbing Blake by the throat and dropping him into the water below. Once they landed in the water, Gio was the first one to attack as Blake felt his razor-sharp teeth nailing into his skin like knives. *Got to get myself out of this*. Each of Gio's teeth dug deeper into his skin. With one swift tear, Blake backed away from Gio, the blood spilling into the water. Blake smiled. Surely, the blood would draw the Hammerheads attention, providing an excellent way to get out of this situation…

Sure enough, a massive crowd of Hammerheads gathered together, trying to figure out where the smell was coming from. Blake swam back as far as he could while the Hammerheads ripped Gio apart. Knowing if he stayed in the water too long he was going to be their second bait, Blake swam to the surface of the ocean and transformed back into his human form before heading back to the Hammerhead Headquarters. As far as he was concerned, Gio went from being the best bodyguard he had to the worst threat possible.

He got what he deserved.

***

Tonia flopped down on the bed and exhaled. After the horrible night she'd had with Stin, all she wanted was to vent to her best friend about how rude and inappropriate he had been in her presence. The trial was starting first thing in the morning, and she didn't have a thing on paper. Now she hated herself for arguing with him in the first place.

"I can't do this anymore. I'm seriously thinking about telling Ford to fire me from this team." Tonia got up and walked over to her desk, the seafood almost gone because of Su-Lee's huge appetite. She picked up the pen and pad before slamming it down on the floor and throwing her hands in the air. "How am I ever going to represent someone like him in court?"

Su-Lee swallowed the last portion of the seafood on the plate.

"I can't believe he overheard the conversation between you and Ford. If he was that desperate to find out what was going on, why didn't he ask Ford about it?"

Tonia rolled her eyes.

"You know what I'm still having a hard time believing? That you two actually slept together."

Memories of their one-night stand flooded through her mind. For the last couple of days, Tonia's dreams altered back and forth between wishing to take Stin's clothes off and having sex with him again and being attacked by another Hammerhead…which ultimately ended with Stin rescuing her and carrying her to his bed…

Hate him already.

"I mean, you two couldn't stand to be in the same room together. If poison and ice came together in a fight, the whole world would be a mess!" she stated.

Tonia sat down on the bed.

"Su-Lee, what am I going to do? I can't be around someone who is constantly spying on me like this."

Su-Lee stared at the ceiling as she leaned across the beautiful oak wood table Tonia designed herself after her first year of training at the Truson School for Shapeshifters.

"Oh!" She nodded.

"Oh, what?" Tonia followed her friend's gaze to the ceiling but didn't see anything. With one swift movement, Su-Lee moved her feet and stood.

"Him spying on you might actually be a good thing." Tonia opened her mouth to say something but got cut off when Su-Lee put her finger to her lips. "I know you are more than capable of taking care of yourself, but I don't think you are aware of just how dangerous these people are. The Hammerhead Squad has been around for years. They are known for killing everyone and everything in sight, and despite whatever issues you two may have at the moment, I am grateful he was there to tackle that horrible Hammerhead guy." Tonia took a deep breath and opened the window, surprised by the gentle breeze sweeping her face. The smell of seawater hung in the air as she imagined the taste of fish marinating on her tongue.

"So, what are you telling me, Su-Lee? You think I still need to stick to this arrangement even though I hate his guts?" Tonia wondered if that last statement was true as she replayed the scene of Stin hitting the unknown assailant in the jaw and how turned on she was by it. Ugh! Why couldn't she turn off her sexual desires for a man she was supposed to hate? The thought released her mind when Su-Lee gently put a hand on her shoulder and stared out the window beside her.

"I think that despite what he did, he was only doing it to protect you from our enemies. Technically, that's what he's supposed to do. Hell, that's what we're all supposed to do," Su-Lee said. Su-Lee turned to her best friend and gave her a playful shove.

Tonia smiled. She missed talking out her problems with her BFF. Tonia remembered how much of an outcast she was after she turned into an Orman. No one wanted to come near her because of where she was from. They thought Tonia was the wild one out of the pack because of the powers she had. The only two people ever close to her heart were Su-Lee and Ford. After she confessed her feelings to Ford, she admitted their relationship hadn't been the same.

"Since we are off the subject of hating Stin for eavesdropping, I think it's time you started talking about the one-night stand you had with him." Su-Lee pushed up her glasses and made herself comfortable by lying down on the bed.

"You're kidding me, right?"

Su-Lee sat up.

"Tonia, I spend twelve hours a day sitting at a computer figuring out codes and monitoring the buildings to make sure no intruders are screwing up our systems with their revenge plots of mass destruction. The only entertainment I get throughout the entire day is playing with online adult gamers where I can create my own virtual world and have sex with whoever I want online." Tonia opened her mouth to speak, but Su-Lee wouldn't stop talking.

"So pardon me if I seem a little too eager to hear about your sex life considering I basically don't have one of my own." Su-Lee pushed her hair back with her hand. "Boy, was that a lot to get off my chest." She turned and sat back down on the bed and kicked off her shoes before she flopped down on the pillow.

"Now come over here and tell me what you can remember from this one-night stand. I want all of the juicy details so I can go to sleep dreaming I was you," she said.

"You do know how pathetic you sound, don't you?"

"Will you please stop patronizing me and get on with the story."

Tonia threw her hands up in the air and lay next to her friend.

"I don't remember that much considering how drunk I was. But I do remember the great sex."

"Did you guys do all three?"

Tonia blushed. Usually, she would be more relaxed when it came to these types of situations. She remembered the numerous nights she'd spent telling Su-Lee about her wild fantasies of Ford ripping her clothes off and throwing her on the bed just to make passionate love to her. This time, it wasn't a fantasy. She'd had a one-night stand with a man she despised.

So why did this feel so different?

"I don't remember," she finally said, knowing Su-Lee was eventually going to ask her again for the answer.

"What do you mean, you don't remember? You have to remember the sex. People always remember the sex when they're drunk."

Tonia agreed. For the last couple of nights, that was all she could think about.

"Well, I don't." She hoped Su-Lee wouldn't press the subject further and was relieved when she saw her friend fast asleep. Tonia felt herself falling asleep but fought the urge by getting out of bed and walking to her desk. She rubbed her eyes and began thinking about her opening statement. Nothing. She hit her pen on the legal pad.

The total jackass you see before you took advantage of my opportunity to get drunk so he could finally get laid.

She slammed the pen down. She knew she was going to be in big trouble if she didn't come up with *something.* She grabbed her cell. Eleven forty-five PM. The trial started at nine in the morning. All she needed was a couple of hours of sleep. If she could at least get four hours, she would be able to get up early enough to have some idea of what she was going to present to the jury.

Provided she didn't have wild fantasies about Stin in the process.

Tonia shook the thought out of her head and wondered what Ford and Stin were doing with Lex. She heard voices outside but didn't try to resolve the situation considering Lex's feelings toward her. Besides, she was still upset with Stin for spying on her. As much as she wanted to focus on anything else, she couldn't help but wonder what those two were doing at the moment. Tonia stared out of the window and watched as the stars glistened in the night sky. She finished her opening statement before she put the pen down and flicked off her desk light. She lay down in her bed and was about to fall asleep when she heard her cell buzzing.

"Hello?" she waited on a response before she repeated her statement.

"The next time I see you or the rest of the team hanging around my family, I won't hesitate to kill you all," the voice said.

CHAPTER EIGHT

Stin sprinted out of the water and landed hard on the sand. The particles flared his nostrils, causing him to cough. His loud coughing fit was interrupted by a loud thump next to him. He didn't have to look to figure out who it was. He rolled over on his back to catch his breath.

"I'll admit I'm not much of a surfing fan, but that was a lot of fun." Ford dusted off the sand and flipped his brown hair back before putting on his clothes. Stin followed suit.

"So, have you calmed down enough to talk about it, or do we have to go surfing again?"

Stin knew the answer. The anger he'd felt earlier in the day about what happened between Tonia and the unsuspecting hammerhead was lessening due to his favorite pastime.

The first part was him and Ford surfing the waves and trying to see who would ride the farthest. Stin beat him. When it was time for them to eat, both decided to turn into their alter egos and grab a bite before resurfacing again. Stin knew he had cooled down, but he still wasn't ready for the night to end. He wanted to go to his favorite place and forget about what went on for the last couple of days.

"No more surfing. Dude, I'm just ready to chill out at one of my favorite bars tonight." Stin headed toward Nise's Bar and Grill, which sat on the other side of the island. He didn't make it too far before Ford gave him a quick tug from behind.

"Don't you think we should call it a night? You're gonna have to get up early in the morning for the trial..."

"Dude, please don't lecture me about this trial. I know you're my boss and everything, but I just need a night of hanging out with my best friend." Stin felt like he was on top of the world and didn't need anyone to make him think otherwise. Now all he needed was a drink and maybe a little fun in-between the sheets.

Ford shrugged.

"All right, just one more hour and then I got to get home. Mandy's probably going to be calling me, asking me where I have been."

Stin opened the door and walked inside to a full crowd of people at the bar and every table available. He cursed once he realized what time of the year it was and made his way to the bar. Luckily, he was able to find two chairs so they could make themselves comfortable. Stin began tapping on the table.

"Hey, can we get some drinks up here?"

"Seriously, why do you do that? You know they are coming to greet us," Ford said.

Stin searched for the one person who always annoyed him about his past sexual experiences. Normally, he would hate to see her come his way, but tonight was different. He needed the distraction. He wanted her to come to him and insult him like he was the worst man on earth.

Stin started reflecting on the last time he had sex with a woman. Tonia came to mind. He still remembered his body on top of hers as they moved to a rhythm all their own. Who needed music in the room when the sexual energy was trapped inside them, waiting for both to explode like never before?

No Dude, we're not doing this again, not tonight.

"Can I help you?" A short brunette girl approached the bar.

"Where's Nise? Is she working tonight?"

The girl shrugged.

"I don't know. She hasn't shown up for the last couple of days."

"Is she okay?" Ford asked, raising a brow.

"Dude, I was going to ask the same question." Stin didn't want to hear any bad news about anyone tonight. He wanted to have some fun but knew that if any of his friends were in danger, his sense of fun would become secondary to saving people's lives.

"They say she just up and left. There was some sort of emergency with her family."

"Do you know when she's coming back?" Stin asked. The smell of burritos and french fries fluttered through the room and landed on the counter a few feet down the bar.

The brunette shrugged again.

"I don't know." She paused. "Look, I just started working here. She told me to fill in for her, and I did."

Stin decided it was best not to interrogate the girl anymore. She seemed annoyed they were even asking her questions in the first place.

"We're sorry for all the questions. We are her friends and just want to know if she's okay. Is there any way we can contact her?" Ford asked.

Stin knew he was trying to reach her but knew it wasn't going to be very successful based on the girl's reaction to the whole situation. The girl shook her head, no. That was good enough for him.

"Can we have a glass of scotch please?" He needed a drink after his latest fantasy of him and Tonia lingered in his brain.

"Sure, coming right up," she said. Stin wanted to order something else but decided against it at the moment.

"Why did you send her away? I needed to know if Nise was safe. Who knows what kind of danger she's in?"

The girl passed the two glasses in their direction.

"Just give the girl a break. If I know Nise, she's probably out with her family in another country somewhere."

Ford's eyebrows closed together.

"Look, if it will help you feel any better, we'll call her first thing." Stin loved hanging out with Ford ever since they first turned into Ormans ten years ago.

For as long as he had known him, Ford was always the one that worried about everyone he came across. While he commended his friend and boss for being concerned about the team, right now he wanted his friend to relax and drink a scotch with him and forget about rescuing everyone who he thought was in trouble. Stin seriously thought Ford read his mind as he gulped down the first glass of scotch.

"So, let's talk about the situation between you and Tonia."

Stin banged his glass down on the table.

"I'd rather not. All I really want to do is drink and forget about her and—" Stin wasn't able to finish the sentence as he saw a dark-skinned woman glide across the room. "—What better way to do that than—"

"—Seriously, Stin? You just slept with Tonia and now you want to sleep with someone else?"

Stin saw how upset Ford was about the whole situation. A part of him regretted taking his best friend to Nise's Bar and Grill because of his sole intention—to get Tonia out of his system. The only way he would be able to do it was if he slept with another woman.

"Ford, trust me. It's better if I get her out of my system now. If I do, then I will be able to focus on the trial."

"No Stin. We have to deal with this. You're running away from what the real problem is, and we have to fix it."

"Really? And what problem is that?" Stin never took his eyes off of the woman during the whole conversation. The way she looked was enough for him to approach her, but he had a feeling Ford was going to dampen his moment.

"That you're starting to have feelings for her like I did with Mandy," Ford announced.

Stin accidentally spit out the last of his scotch onto the countertop and started laughing. "Ford, my man." Stin hit him across the back. "Normally, I would agree with you on many things, but this time you're wrong."

"Am I?" Ford raised a brow. "Let me ask you something Stin. Did you follow Tonia out there on the island or did you just so happen to be there at the right place at the right time as they say?" The smugness in Ford's voice got under Stin's skin. He and Tonia together? As in a couple? There was no way they could ever possibly be together. They hated each other…couldn't stand the sight of each other. On the other side of the equation, Stin wouldn't mind sleeping with her again.

And you can't stand the sight of her? Be serious.

"It's the only thing that makes sense. Why else would you go and rescue the one person you despise? Why is it any of your business she told me everything that happened today instead of you?"

Stin pondered the questions in his mind while staring at the woman for the hundredth time. She managed to look his way and smile while she leaned in and whispered something to another woman sitting next to her.

"I had to save her life Stin. That jackass hammerhead was going to kill her. I needed to save her so you wouldn't have one less team member on your hands." Before Ford could open his mouth and defend his argument, Stin went on. "Even if we did have a fling, there would never be any chance it would go beyond that."

Ford took another sip of his drink and gawked at him. Stin tried to ignore it by staring at the woman. Unfortunately, the woman had moved to the other side of the bar and had been replaced by a tall chubby blonde woman walking toward him.

"I'm waiting," Ford said, snapping him out of his quest.

Stin grunted.

"Ford, if you're not going to let me have some fun tonight, then the least you can do is leave." A surge of ice rushed through his veins. He didn't want to deal with Ford's absurd comments about his feelings for Tonia anymore, especially since he knew it wasn't the truth.

Or was it?

Okay, so maybe he wanted to relive the intense sex he'd experienced the other night with her, and maybe he did dream about which position he had her in. As much as he hated to admit it, the sex was good between them. But that sure as hell didn't mean he wanted anything more than sex.

"Hello." While Stin was deep in thought about Tonia, the chubby woman approached the bar. Stin watched as Ford took one last swig of scotch and stood. He grabbed his jacket.

"Stin, you were the one that stated you needed to have some fun with me tonight. We did your favorite activity then you invited me to Nise's just to hang out. I thought maybe we could talk about your true feelings for

Tonia, but if you don't want to talk about it, then I won't force it." Ford tossed the money on the table. He turned to the woman. "Hope you have a great time with him."

Stin prayed he wouldn't say anything else to make the woman believe he was some sort of player who just wanted to sleep with her to relieve the sexual tension lurking in his mind for the last few hours. A sense of relief flooded through him when Ford headed out the door without saying a word. Stin reached for the glass but to his disappointment, found it to be empty.

"I can fill that glass for you," the woman replied. She had a difficult time sitting down on the seat but managed to sustain her weight once she got comfortable. Stin admitted to himself this woman wasn't his first choice but decided it was best not to completely dismiss the idea. After what he'd been through, maybe it was time for him to try something different. Something new.

"Chi-Chi, can you give us two more refills please?"

Chi Chi winked.

"Coming right up."

"So, what's a woman like you doing in a bar like this?" he asked, trying to sound as charming as he could.

The woman smiled.

"I decided to go out for once instead of sitting at home." She wanted to say more but restrained herself. "What is your sexy ass doing in the bar this late at night?"

Stin was surprised by the bold remark.

"Uh—" *I'm here because I was looking to find a woman who I could get drunk with, take home, and screw until she screams my name in ecstasy.*

"Are you there?" The woman waved her hand in front of him. Stin cursed. The night was starting to get very dull. He needed to release what had been growing inside him since his one-night stand with the woman he couldn't stand the sight of.

"What do you say we get out of here and head back to my place?" He downed the last glass of scotch and scooted himself off the stool. The smell of steak and Cajun fries filled his nostrils, reminding him he needed to cook a lovely dinner for him and his new guest once he arrived at his cabin.

"Sure," she said, smiling at the invitation. Stin helped her get down off of the stool. He threw his money on the counter before escorting the woman outside. The sun settled behind the beautiful waves of the ocean, causing a magnificent view of what the island truly represented, love and beauty.

"What's your name?" The woman asked as they walked down the sandy shores.

"I'm Stin," he said, hoping he didn't have to reveal his full identity.

"As in Stin Vanderson?"

His heart stopped. He felt the ice trickling down his body. Maybe it was a bad idea to bring her to his cabin. If anyone found out about his true identity, the entire team would be screwed and the higher-ups would do whatever it took to destroy him.

"How do you know my name?" he asked. He felt the lump forming in his throat.

"Lots of women have been talking about you and your one-night stands." *Shit.* He was screwed. He exhaled when she didn't mention his alter ego. Unfortunately, it was replaced by a feeling of dread.

"I guess you're just not into that type of stuff, huh?" he guessed. "Look, I understand if want to back out of the deal."

"Not at all," she replied, shaking her head no. She inched closer to him. "It's quite the opposite. I love one-night stands."

Stin's eyes bulged. "Really?"

She nodded.

"What exactly do you like about them?"

"I love meeting strangers and having sex with them. I would hope it turns into a relationship, but if it doesn't…"

The woman shrugged. Clearly, this woman wasn't serious about her one-night affairs? Stin had a feeling she was making conversation to avoid feeling the rejection once it was all over. "Tonight is no different."

Stin nodded and approached his cabin. He let the woman go inside to explore the view before he walked inside, took off his jacket and headed for the kitchen. He opened the fridge and took out the steak he had bought a couple of days ago and grabbed a skillet from the cabinet.

"You have a beautiful place here."

"Thank you." He focused his attention on the steak before going back to the fridge again. He stared at all the choices in front of him and decided it was best to let the woman decide what she wanted.

"With your steak, do you want mash potatoes? Rice?…"

"Mashed potatoes would be great thanks."

Stin grabbed a couple of potatoes and the vegetable peeler.

"How long have you been living here?"

"Years. At least ten or more. I lost count after three." He searched the inside of the cabinet and grabbed the salt.

"So, are you married? Do you have any children?"

"No." Stin reflected on the question while stirring the potatoes. Marriage and children never entered his mind.

"Would you like to get married and have children someday?"

Stin shrugged.

"Maybe." The answer disturbed him. All his adult life had been about was one-night stands, half of which he couldn't even remember. He couldn't help but imagine what his life would be like with marriage and children.

"Would you like to have it with me someday?" The woman rubbed his back.

Stin lifted his head. He didn't have time to answer the woman's question as the woman planted her lips on his. He felt her tongue press against his with such fury it knocked him off balance. Despite her good intentions, all he could think about was how much he wanted to be with Tonia…how much he wanted her tongue massaging his…how he wanted to massage every curve of her body while their bodies mingled between the bedsheets. Once the kiss ended, the woman's face had morphed into Tonia's hazel brown eyes and magnificent cheekbones. The woman leaned toward him.

"How was that for you?" She rubbed her hands against his. "Why don't we leave the food and head upstairs?" She lifted a brow. Stin cleared his throat.

"Listen." He tried to think of the woman's name, but nothing came to mind.

"Tanya," she said. They were so close to each other that Stin felt her stomach pushing against his.

"Tanya, I'm grateful you decided to stay and talk. I mean, it was great I got to know you and everything, but I don't think anything is going to happen tonight." She stepped back. Stin swallowed hard. Frankly, he couldn't believe it himself. He was turning down an offer—usually, he would have her in his bed by now. The whole scenario took him by surprise.

"You mean to tell me you got me all the way over here to your place just to turn me down?"

It didn't make sense to him either.

"I'm sorry you feel that way. I didn't think the night was going to end like this, but unfortunately, I don't think it's going to work out," he said. He knew there wasn't going to be a next time. Stin knew what he wanted much more than he ever thought possible and he knew Tanya wasn't what he was looking for. He wanted the one person he thought he hated for the longest time. Never in a million years did he think he would admit he wanted Tonia all over again.

That was the scariest and most exciting part of all.

"Since we're not going to sleep together tonight, is it too much to ask if I have a decent meal before I head out? I'm starving. I wanted to eat at the grill, but my best friend bailed on me, and I didn't have enough money for the steak."

Stin didn't mind the invitation. Hell, he needed the distraction after everything that had happened tonight. It was only fair to give the woman a decent meal after being turned down for sex, right?

Problem was, he wasn't supposed to be in the cabin at all. The Hammerheads could have killed both of them on the spot, and no one would come to their rescue until they were both lying down on the floor, with their hearts and guts torn out. What the hell was he thinking dragging Tanya here tonight?

"Tell you what, why don't I cook you the meal and you can take it with you?" he asked.

The smile dropped into a frown.

"Why? It's like you're getting rid of me or something. Do you have another bitch on the side?"

There was the anger Stin was trying to avoid. She was twice his size and despite the huge muscles he'd obtained ever since he turned into his alter ego a decade ago, he still wasn't a match for a three-hundred-pound woman. Besides, his parents always taught him never to hit any woman no matter what they said or did.

Not that he had that intention anyway…

"It's not like that. I'm a…" Stin tried to think of a perfect excuse that sounded believable. "Cop. I have criminals coming after me…really horrible criminals." Stin only gave a small token of opportunity for her to respond before he went on. "I don't want to see you in danger. If they find out I'm here, they'll kill us both." He liked the lie. It was partly true, and it wasn't too much of a stretch except for his powers—something in which she didn't need to know.

"Oh, wow. I didn't know it was that serious. Do you have time to cook all this stuff?"

"Yeah. No one knows we're here yet. I'm just going to cook the food really quick and send a plate home with you," Stin said. The second part of the comment seemed a little far-fetched, but he didn't want to be some rude ass jerk kicking the woman out because he was no longer interested in having an affair with her. He also couldn't risk her knowing who he truly was.

Tanya sighed.

"No, that's okay. I'll go back to the grill and buy something there. I had a taste for their French fries anyway."

Stin could tell she was lying but didn't want to push the issue. If the woman wanted to leave, then he had no choice but to accept that request. It would be better for both of them anyway.

The woman stood up.

"By the way, who is the lucky girl grabbing your attention?" she asked.

"What?"

The woman held her hands up.

"Please don't insult me. I've been through this too many times with too many men. When they don't want to sleep with me, I know it's because of someone else, so who is it?"

Stin hesitated. He had to admit Tanya was one of the smartest women he knew. He felt guilty about what he had done to her. Ford was right, this whole one-night stand thing was a big mistake on his part.

"She's someone I thought I didn't like for the longest time. I used to hate everything there was about her—her look, the way she dressed, the way she used to barge in whenever I was working on something or even when she just needed the boss for something—she used to use me to send messages to him."

"What kind of messages?" she asked.

Stin shrugged.

"Mostly business. I used to hate the way she lusted after him, though. I thought it was so unprofessional." He paused. "But now, I think I get it."

"You must really be in love with her then."

There went that word again. The one word Stin had been dreading since their story between him and Tonia began. Even the word love was enough to make him cringe.

"I'm not in love with her," he said, dismissing the statement completely. "I just don't hate her as much as I used to."

"And why is that?"

Stin wanted to fire back that it was none of her business. Who was she to ask all of these questions when she hardly knew who he was? He replayed what she stated over in his mind.

"There's more to her than I ever imagined." *Stop talking,* he told himself. *You've already given her enough information. Don't do something you'll regret later on.* "Listen, it's getting late and I really need to get out of here before my cover gets blown."

She waved it off.

"I get it. I'm leaving." She got up from hcr chair and gawked at him before she stuck her hand out. "It was nice meeting you anyway."

Stin shook it.

"It was nice meeting you too," he replied. A part of him wanted to extend the invitation to a home-cooked meal for the company, but there were too many things he needed to focus on and having a conversation with another woman knowing she would be in danger was not an option. Stin escorted Tanya to the door.

"Before we both decide to never see each other again, I really think you should tell whoever that woman is how you feel. You never know," she said.

Stin didn't say another word, just watched the woman go out the door. He thought about what the woman had said but decided that now wasn't going to be a good time to announce his feelings for Tonia.

There was too much going on. He needed to focus on keeping Lex and Tonia safe. He stared at the clock and cursed himself for not following his right mind and ending the night with Ford and him surfing. It was too late now. He needed to focus on what was important at this moment.

Stin went back into the kitchen. Despite the distraction with Tanya, he still managed to cook everything in a timely fashion. As he sat down in the chair and ate, all he could think about was Tonia and Lex. He knew he needed to have a discussion with Lex about the living arrangements with him and Tonia. Considering all of the drama that occurred last year, he understood how Lex felt. He needed Lex to try and get along with her for his sake.

Which he knew was going to be an uphill battle.

CHAPTER NINE

"Tonia? Tonia, you're going to be late for the trial. *Tonia, wake up!*" The violent shaking caused Tonia to jump and face whoever was waking her up. Considering the awful night she'd had between the mysterious phone call and staying up until the wee hours of the morning writing her opening statement, she didn't get enough sleep. She was on the verge of attacking the person when she realized the person who woke her up was none other than her best friend Su-Lee, who was now resisting the attack by putting her hands up.

"Hey, don't kill the messenger, okay? You're late for the trial…"

"…No, I'm not," Tonia said, cutting her off and looking at the time. "The trial starts at nine a.m."

"It's past nine, Tonia. It's ten a.m. I've been trying to wake you up for the last hour."

Tonia cursed. She grabbed her cell and looked at the time. Sure enough, she was an hour late for the trial, which meant she was already on the judge's bad side from the very start. Where the hell was Stin? He needed to be at the trial on time, or else it could ruin his chances with the jury based on his behavior alone.

"You're going to be okay, Tonia. Just throw something on and head straight out the door." Su-Lee put on her glasses and started smelling herself. "Just make sure you don't end up smelling like me in the process."

Tonia flew open the doors to her closet and threw clothes out on the bed. Su-Lee's comment seemed promising now that she knew she was strapped for time.

"Are you ready to go?" a voice said from the door. Tonia jumped. Her alter ego responded, ready for an attack. She took a deep breath when she saw it was only Stin standing in the doorway.

"I think that's my cue to leave." Su-Lee grabbed her purse off of the dresser. "I'll see you guys at the trial." Before Tonia could mutter another sound, Su-Lee was out the door, leaving Tonia and Stin standing alone, facing each other.

Stin looked at his watch.

"You're running a little late this morning. Do you have anything to wear for court?" he asked. Tonia focused on the wardrobe he wore and couldn't help but sigh. The dark black suit with the right tie along with his sparkling blue eyes would make any woman swoon.

"I see you're all dressed up for the trial. I'm surprised you managed to make it in. What time did you get here?" Tonia asked, wanting to take the words back. What right did she have to question who he was screwing? They had one night together, that was it. As Stin inched closer, Tonia could smell the body wash cascading through his skin. Her alter ego stirred. The smell of him was enough for her body to go from zero to one hundred degrees in a matter of seconds.

Get it together. You need to focus on the trial.

"Why are you asking? Considering how upset you were about what I did yesterday, I thought maybe you didn't care."

"I don't." She took off her pajamas, leaving nothing but her underwear.

Stin cleared his throat.

What the hell was she doing? It wasn't enough that she had the best sex she ever dreamed of despite her drunken state. Now she was undressing in front of him like…

A couple?

"Don't mind me, I'm just enjoying the view. Feel free to do whatever you want. It's your house, after all." The eyebrow raise in addition to the smug attitude he carried when it came to that last statement made her shiver.

"What's going on?" he asked. There was no way she was going to give him what he wanted to hear. She didn't want to believe it herself but knew what she had to do to eliminate the tension between them. "Why did you jump out of your skin like that?" After a few seconds of trying to put on deodorant, Tonia covered herself up in matching black jacket and skirt.

"Because the thought of you and me sleeping together will never happen. It happened once, that's it. The last thing I need is more drama," she said. She went to the mirror to fix her hair before she grabbed her jacket and purse. "Let's go."

Once they made eye contact, Stin's expression changed. His confidence was shattered. Tonia hate doing it to him, but it was the only thing she could think of to make their so-called "business partnership" stay where it needed to be. As Tonia headed to the door, Stin moved out of the way without a word, his cold blue eyes giving Tonia the notion that what she'd said had struck a chord. She felt her heart beating and sweat form around her forehead as they jumped into the Ford Escalade parked in the back of the cabin and headed off to the courthouse.

Stin turned the corner and drove out onto the road without saying a word. The silence should have been a welcoming experience for both of them. Unfortunately, it wasn't. She wanted to apologize and tell him she was wrong. She kept reminding herself of the hatred she used to feel for him. It would make the time go by faster if she felt nothing at all.

If only it was the truth...

"So am I really that horrible? Do you hate me so much you would rather die than sleep with me?" he asked, turning the corner.

Tonia checked the time. That hour and a half looked worse by the minute.

"Don't you feel the same about me?" She waited for him to confirm what she already knew. Silence filled the air between them before Stin opened his mouth.

"No. Not anymore."

Tonia closed her eyes and swallowed hard. She heard her own heartbeat thumping against her chest as they finally parked in front of the courthouse. Tonia cursed herself for being a part of this arrangement while Stin held the door open for her to walk inside.

Tonia turned.

"By the way, I just thought you should know…" She cut herself off when Stin walked down the hallway. She wanted to remind him about them not walking in together in the courtroom, but it seemed like Stin had already gotten the message as his slick black shoes scraped against the black-tiled floor and proceeded inside. Tonia straighten herself up and headed in, knowing the judge wasn't too happy with her tardiness. To her surprise, several people had already arrived in the courtroom, anxiously waiting for the trial to start. Tonia's eyes locked on the two hammerheads who may have possibly threatened her life and Stin's.

Anger filled her veins as she walked by and took her place at the table on the other side of the courtroom.

"Ms. Ojai, there better be a really good explanation of why you're an hour and a half late," the judge barked.

"I apologize your honor. I was under the impression the trial started at ten a.m., not nine." She hoped the judge wasn't going to go down hard on her. She needed to prove to the jury and the judge she was capable of representing her client, and he was innocent of all the charges the Hammerheads accused him of.

"There is no excuse for tardiness Ms. Ojai. The next time it happens, your case will be dismissed."

"I understand your honor," she said. She exhaled. "Permission to present my opening statement?"

The judge shifted in his seat.

"You may but just know that the prosecution has already presented their side."

Tonia cursed. They already had the upper hand by convincing the jury the evidence they needed to make Stin look guilty of the crime. *Hate them.* She gathered her paperwork together and started on her opening statement.

***

Stin heard the echo of Tonia's voice flow throughout the courtroom and couldn't help but give her props on her statement. She seemed to be on a roll despite both of them being tardy. Just a few minutes before Tonia walked in, the judge gave him a good lecture on tardiness as well, something he didn't take too well but knew better than to fight with someone who held the verdict on whether he should live or die. Besides, his mind wasn't focused on the trial, his mind focused on Tonia's comment before the trial started. Usually, he would blow it off, but this time felt different.

Did she even realize how close he'd been to screwing another woman? How much he'd tried to hide the emotions he felt as he watched the other women at the bar?

The judge banged on the gavel.

"I have heard both parties when it comes to this matter." The judge paused. "I'm ordering the suspect to be under surveillance for now. Considering he's a part of the Truson S.E.T., he will need to be monitored by one of the team's personal security until tomorrow."

"But your honor…"

"I have reached my decision." The judge slammed the gavel. "Now, before we decide to end the trial, the jury members will stand up one by one and introduce themselves. Once that happens, we will resume the trial early tomorrow morning at nine a.m. Everyone is expected to be on time. Failure will result in the trial being dismissed and everyone being held in contempt. Does everyone understand these rules?"

"Yes, your honor," they both stated. Ice boiled in Stin's arms as he watched Blake and his lawyer. After everything he'd pulled on Stin, he wanted to kill him the same way he did when one of his Hammerhead crew attempted to kill Tonia. He knew he was innocent of these charges and hated that Blake and his wife stood there, smug and arrogant, confident about him being guilty of a crime he didn't commit. The ice grew thicker on the inside, causing him to focus on the rest of the jury members to calm himself down.

Stin watched as all of the members of the jury introduced themselves. A horrible sense of dread and anger filled his mind. Stin couldn't help but search through each of the jury members' faces in his head. Half he recognized. His mind replayed the conversation he'd had at the hospital with Ford. He gave the jury members one final look. They all looked familiar, but he couldn't understand why.

"Thank you to the jury members for introducing yourselves to the prosecutors and defense. This trial will officially begin tomorrow morning." The judge banged his gavel and stood up.

Then it hit Stin. The worst thought he could ever imagine went through his head. Was Tonia setting him up for death? It would make sense; she did hate his guts and stated she didn't want anything more than a business partnership.

Confront her stupid.

Stin got up from the chair and stared at the woman who represented him in court. In one way, it didn't make sense she was bending over backwards to represent him other than the fact that she was forced into it by their boss. On the other hand, it could have been a cover-up to hide what she was doing—getting revenge for every horrible thing he had ever said or done to her.

"Tonia!" he called out as Tonia made her way out the door. She turned to face him while keeping her hand on the door. "We need to talk." Another jury member excused himself before heading out into the hallway. Tonia's hands escaped the grips of the door as she carefully walked up to Stin.

"What?"

"You stated that we are nothing more than business partners correct?" he asked.

"Yes."

"Then I need you to be honest with me and tell me what you're up to," he said.

Tonia took a step back.

"What are you talking about?"

"I'm talking about you setting me up." Before Tonia could speak, Stin pointed to the rows of chairs that were now empty. "Those jury members—I know them, Tonia—they look and sound familiar."

Tonia shrugged.

"If you know something I don't, then by all means share," she said.

Stin could hear the bitterness in her voice. Poison raged in her eyes. The conversation was now turning back to the beginning, where they were becoming enemies once again. He inched closer but she stood tall, ready for a fight.

"Tonia, the jury members are not impartial. All of those members belong to the Hammerhead Squad."

"And you think I would be a part of that? You think I would set you up with the Hammerhead Squad of all people after what happened yesterday in the ocean?"

Stin thought about it. It didn't make sense. Why would Tonia go through all of the trouble?

"Do you seriously know what you are accusing me of?"

"I'm sorry," he said. "I should have thought about what I said before I said it. It's just that—"

"—I wouldn't do anything that would jeopardize my reputation as a lawyer or as a member of the Truson S.E.T. Besides, what good will it do to the rest of the team if you are sent to prison for a crime you didn't commit?" Despite the reassurance, Stin couldn't help but wonder how *she* would feel about him going to jail for a crime he didn't commit. He tried to distract himself from the mixed feelings he had when it came to her, but things only got worse when he glanced at the outfit she was wearing and how she looked earlier while she got dressed…

"So, if we have nothing more to say to each other, then I'm going to excuse myself and head out the door and get ready for our official first day at the trial," she said.

"Hey Tonia, did you get the message? You are to come bright and early tomorrow morning. I hope you know that there are no second chances when it comes to these types of situations," a familiar voice said. She stopped and turned on her heel.

"You." She pointed her finger at Blake. "You were the one that called me last night."

"Called you?" Stin repeated. The sexual urges he felt were replaced by anger and curiosity. "What do you mean? What are you talking about?"

"I would like to know the answer to that one myself, considering my client doesn't even know your phone number," Blake's lawyer piped in. "My client was with me discussing some legal issues on this trial."

Stin felt the ice forming again. This was the second time he was out of the loop when it came to the Hammerhead's threats. The whole thing was really starting to piss him off. This business partnership wasn't going the way he wanted. He had a duty and a responsibility to protect the people he cared about, but Tonia made it hard for him to do much of anything.

"You know, you really should stop making up stories as you go along. It could damage your credibility," Blake said. Blake let out a sly grin as another pair of heels clicked hard against the tiled floor. "I would suggest you save your prayers for what's gonna happen next *Stin.* You better hope your ancestors can bail you out of this one."

"You bastard!" a woman screamed. She pulled her arm back, her hand almost landed on Stin's face, but Blake grabbed the woman, shielding her from the blow.

"Jessica, no!" A whiff of her short curly wig flowed in the other direction, revealing her true identity. After struggling for only a few seconds, the top of her head turned into the odd shape of a hammer. Stin stood in disbelief. He knew it was possible for any Orman to transform into an orca, but their bodies had to be inside water for that to happen.

Or else they were dead.

But this transformation seemed to happen without hesitation…something that took him by surprise. Stin focused his attention on Tonia who seemed just as surprised as he was about the transformation.

"You son of a bitch, you don't deserve to live!" Jessica snarled at Stin.

"Jessica, stop! You're gonna die like this!" Blake said.

"Get off of me! I want him to pay for what he's done to my brother!"

"What do you want me to do?" Blake's lawyer asked.

"You come anywhere near me or my family, and I will make sure everything you ever worked for will be destroyed," Stin said.

"Oh well, I think that was a threat, did I hear that right?" Blake's lawyer asked.

Blake pointed to his lawyer.

"Take Jessica out of here right now."

Jessica continued to wiggle herself free from his lawyer's grasp as she took another swipe at Stin. She missed his face, but her nails scraped up against Tonia's cheek, and she screamed as her nails made contact with Tonia's powers, each nail sizzling to the ground in a fury of green mush.

"How does it feel?" Tonia asked. "Does the pain hurt at all?"

Stin let out a sly grin while Blake yelled at his lawyer to take control of the situation. Once the lawyer escorted Jessica out of the courtroom, Blake's jaw clenched in anger.

"Both of you are gonna pay for what you did to Jojo and John."

"Bring it on." Stin wanted to send him flying across the room with one fist to the face but decided against it. He knew one wrong move would send him to prison for a long time and would make it look like he was the guilty party for killing Jojo. As much as he wanted to knock Blake dead, he couldn't. Not here. There were too many witnesses.

"Let's go," Tonia said, ushering Stin toward the door.

Blake raised a brow.

"I think you should listen to your *lawyer*," Blake mocked.

Stin didn't bother to turn around while Tonia ushered him outside of the courtroom. Tonia glanced over her shoulder to make sure Blake and his lawyer were around the corner before she pulled Stin to the other side of the hallway.

"What the hell do you think you're doing? Have you lost your mind?"

He knew he shouldn't have done it. He wouldn't have made so many threats if he were in the same position a year ago.

"I know I shouldn't have threatened him, but he shouldn't have mocked me."

Tonia folded her arms.

"What is this, some sort of ego trip? Oh, he mocked me so I'm gonna make threats that could land me behind bars or worse?"

"I'm not going to apologize for what he said, and I'm sure as hell not apologizing for his wife putting her hands on you. I refuse."

"Why? Why are you making this so difficult for me to do my job and represent you?" The fire raging in her eyes was enough to drive him insane. He grabbed her by the shoulders and pulled her close to him. His lips pressed hard against hers, the heat surging through them while their tongues mingled in a passion of fury.

This was what he craved. He *needed* her to fulfill whatever sexual desires were coursing through his body. Stin imagined the sweet smell of tangerines as he rubbed his hands up and down her back, her breasts rubbing against his chest. Before he got a chance to take her in the middle of the hallway, Tonia pushed him away.

"That's why. I can't stop thinking about you, Tonia." Tonia wiped her face and stared at him. "I know you're starting to feel something for me."

Tonia shook her head.

"This is not happening. I can't do this with you," Tonia said.

"Why not Tonia?"

"Because we are business partners—"

"—I know what you claim we are, but you and I both know it's not true anymore—"

Tonia cut him off by walking toward the double doors of the building. Anger engulfed him as he strutted after her. So this was how she wanted to settle this? *No. This isn't how I wanted to resolve this.* Stin stormed after her and realized they had ridden together to the courthouse. Clearly, she wouldn't drive off in the truck without him?

This is Tonia, Stin. What fantasy world are you living in? She probably hates you now more than ever. Stin gained speed while Tonia headed toward the truck. He needed to stop her and get things out in the open. She was able to say how she felt without his input, now it was time for his voice to be heard.

He needed to tell her how he felt—once and for all.

***

Lex breathed a sigh of relief. It had been the first time he finally felt free ever since Ford decided to lock him up at the Truson Headquarters after his disagreement with Stin. He couldn't believe Stin's betrayal. Stin getting along with the one woman who tried to destroy him and his friends?

Never.

"So, what do you think we should do, man? Our boy is stuck in the house with nothing to do because he doesn't like the wicked witch of the west?" Jamie's voice echoed through the island as he took another swig of his beer.

"Not anymore," Lex said. Teven and Jamie turned and gave Lex a well-deserved hug. It felt good to be around his buddies again after their whole ordeal with Ford and Stin.

"Hey man, how did you get out of being in that lab for so long?" Teven asked.

Lex didn't want to share the details about what happened. He just wanted to spend the next few hours hanging out with his friends without having to think about Stin's horrible decision to choose a woman who he despised.

"That's not important man. Right now, I just want to hang out with my two best buds and maybe make out with a couple of girls along the way." Lex eyed the girl he'd had a crush on since he first transferred to the Truson School for Shapeshifters as he stood on the edge of the water, giggling at all of her friends who were throwing each other into the water, laughing the whole time.

"Oooh, do you mean you want to holler at Sidney over there?"

"Yeah, I heard she's totally hot," Jamie mocked. Both of them broke out in laughter and high fived each other. Lex didn't care. He welcomed his friends teasing him as long as he didn't have to think about what was going on in his life.

"I'll be right back," Lex said, focusing his attention on the girls. He watched as they slowly moved back from the water until one girl screamed.

Lex ran to where the girls were only to realize what they had seen in the water. A dead man had washed up along the shores of Truson. A man who looked too familiar for his taste…

CHAPTER TEN

"Go get help!" Lex commanded. "This man needs help!" He kept repeating the sentence over again while watching the man's face. His eyes shot open, causing some of the kids to jump back. Lex moved forward and squatted down, never losing eye contact with the man before him.

"What's your name?" Lex asked.

He felt Teven's hand hit him on the shoulder.

"Dude, what the hell man? I think we should head for the hills!" Teven hit him on the shoulder again. "Let's leave him."

"Is that what you guys are supposed to do in an emergency?" Ford asked as he, Su-Lee and Gabriel approached them. "If that's all you learned in classes at the Truson School for Shapeshifters, then I need to reevaluate the teachers."

"I second that," Su-Lee piped in. "What's going on?"

"Gio—vanni," the man spoke. He closed his eyes again, his head slumped to the side of the sand.

"Lex, Teven, Jamie—all of you—go back inside the headquarters right now."

"But what's gonna happen to him?" Lex asked.

"I think we should go back inside and let Ford and the rest of the team handle this," Su-Lee said. She grabbed onto Lex's shoulder, but Lex flinched, flicking Su-Lee's hand away.

"I want to stay out here. Why can't I stay?"

"You know why, Lex. Don't make this situation worse."

"Worse? How can the situation get worse than this? These people are after me and Stin. I almost got killed trying to rescue Stin after they injected that poison into his jaw. I'm not a kid, I can handle it." Lex watched as Ford's hand focused on the man's left side of his ribs before he stood again.

"This man looks like he's half-human, half-shark."

"What do you think that means?" Gabriel asked, staring at the man who was now unconscious. "Should we gather the team?"

"He's probably a Hammerhead…the same Hammerhead that attacked me and Stin the other day. Doesn't anyone listen to me around here?" Lex barked.

The intensity of Ford's eyes deepened as he watched Lex.

"Su-Lee, I want Lex and the rest of the children on this island to be examined, just to be on the safe side. We don't know where this man came from or what kind of diseases might have been spread since he's been here. Go." Su-Lee continued to struggle with Lex.

"Gabriel, help Su-Lee with Lex and his friends and see if you can find the bodyguards in the facility to help me carry this guy back to the lab." Gabriel nodded, and Lex continued to struggle until Gabriel raised his fist and punched him in the jaw. After a few stumbles, Lex fell face first onto the sand.

"Does anyone else need to challenge me just to see how tough you really are?"

"Why did you have to hit him like that?" Teven asked.

Gabriel pushed him toward the building and ushered the rest in.

"I can take care of myself. I don't need you to babysit me all the time."

"That's for us to decide," Su-Lee said. Just as they made it halfway to the laboratory, Tonia and Stin strutted toward them.

"Tonia, aren't we going to talk about this? You can't just run away from everything. Don't you think it's time…" Stin lost focus of Tonia when he saw Lex. He inched closer. "What's going on? Has he been attacked again?"

"Like you care," Lex replied. "All you have ever cared about was her." Lex motioned his head to Tonia, who was now heading closer to the chaos surrounding the island. She closed her eyes and pinched her nose.

"What's going on now? Please tell me it isn't another hammerhead?" Tonia whined as she got closer to the unknown body before them.

"How do you—" Ford cut himself off before he could go any further. "Never mind. How was the trial?"

"We're being set up," Stin said. He bent down and examined the man's body. "Did he say anything yet?"

Ford shrugged.

"I think the guy is dead."

"Do you know what kind of creature he was?" From the way the bones were structured through his ribcage, there could only be two possible guesses—a great white or a hammerhead.

"Couldn't really tell since he was human. His face was barely recognizable. Lex was the one who discovered the body washed up along the shore," Ford said then turned to Tonia. "Tonia?"

A dazed look formed around her face.

"What did you mean when you said you think you are being set-up?" she asked. "Who do you think is setting you up?" Stin extended his arm to the dead body being carried away by the bodyguards.

"Are you seriously asking that question? Look at what's happening Tonia. The Hammerheads keep coming after us. The jury is all controlled by the Hammerhead Squad."

"But there is no proof they are involved." Tonia threw her hands up in the air.

Stin focused on the bodyguards carrying the body to headquarters. He needed to check on Lex to make sure he was okay. The last thing he needed was for Lex to be in any more danger than he was earlier in the week. Stin followed the bodyguards into the building with Tonia coming close behind followed by Su-Lee and Gabriel.

"I agree with Stin. I think the Hammerheads are behind this and that it's time to retaliate," Ford said. "For now, I think Tonia needs to be someplace safe until the man is released into our custody."

"There's no need to worry about Tonia. I'm going to do everything in my power to protect her. Nothing's gonna happen as long as we are living together." Stin watched as Ford and Gabriel looked at each other before Ford broke the silence.

"I think you guys should go back to the house A.S.A.P. and take Lex with you."

"No way," Lex said.

"Until the trial is over, you're not allowed to hang out with your friends. It's too dangerous."

"Why not? I know how to take care of myself. I don't need a babysitter," Lex said. "I should be able to hang out with my friends if I want to."

"It's far too dangerous while the Hammerhead Squad is running wild and killing everything that moves. You have to stay with us until everything is settled."

Stin saw Lex ball his hands into fists.

"This isn't fair. I shouldn't be punished for something someone else did!" Lex threw his arm back and created a boulder the size of his fist and threw it against one of the statues. It clipped one of the orca's fins as it exploded into the air, the dust cascading all over the floor. The team was quick and managed to dodge some of the debris that landed below them. Ford glared at Lex with such anger Stin thought he was going to attack him with his powers.

"I did not appreciate that Lex. I understand you are upset about what's going on but dcstroying our statue—especially the one that truly represents who we are—is completely irresponsible," Ford said. "Pull something like that again, and you will be severely punished."

Lex shrugged, and Stin waited on the confrontation—if he felt like Ford was out of bounds, then he would have to step in to rectify the situation.

"Man, I'm done with this place. Screw you." Lex turned and headed out the door.

Tonia ran after him, surprised by her sudden reaction, but decided to do it anyway. Her efforts were stopped when she felt a warm hand on her shoulder.

"Hang on Tonia. I think it would be best if I talk to him," Stin said and went after him.

Lex turned and saw Stin coming after him and picked up speed. He couldn't believe he was actually being punished for something he had nothing to do with. On top of that, he had to deal with someone who caused him a great deal of stress and anger.

"Lex! Lex!" He could hear Stin calling his name but kept going until he reached the cabin.

He wanted to leave. Leave the island and everything it stood for. He wanted to live life on his terms…not someone else's. If Stin or the rest of the team couldn't understand that, then that was their problem.

***

She wanted to prove she wasn't the horrible monster Stin claimed her to be. For some reason, she wanted everything to work out between Lex and Stin. As far as her and Stin, however, it was a no-brainer. They couldn't work together as a team. Despite how much her body wanted a repeat of what happened, she couldn't risk getting hurt again. However, she ended up feeling worse than before when Stin decided to go after Lex instead of her. She'd hoped she would be able to calm him down and make amends with him, especially since she was the reason why Lex was so angry in the first place. Unfortunately, Stin took that away from her, leaving her with a sense of feeling hopeless.

She didn't like that feeling.

"It's okay. You shouldn't stress out about it, Stin just wanted to be there for Lex, that's all," Su-Lee said.

Tonia swung her hair back.

"Why are you telling me this? I could care less about what is going on between Stin and Lex." Tonia pretended it didn't bother her by shrugging it off. "I'm just hoping there won't be another world war three between us and the Hammerheads before the trial starts." Tonia focused on Ford to minimize the distraction of Stin running after Lex. She also wanted to focus on what she needed to do to stay away from Stin period—especially after the conversation they'd had earlier.

"Well, the best thing we can do is to get as much information on this man whether he is dead or alive." Ford put his hands behind his back and headed toward the body lying in the far corner of the front hallway in a gurney, ready to be taken into the lab for further examination. Tonia wanted to go with him to see if Ford was going to get anything out of the man who could ultimately make or break her case…but decided against it. She needed to let Ford handle it and see if there was anything that could be admissible in court.

Despite the urge, Tonia didn't feel to question Ford about the unnamed man and what he might have possibly said or done before he was discovered or even if the man was alive or dead, she had more than enough excitement for one day. She needed to focus on the information she had now and to get her reputation back with the judge after her tardiness.

"Are you okay? Do we need another girls'-night-in?" Su-Lee bumped her shoulder. Tonia knew what she needed to do despite the way she felt every time Stin got close to her. A part of her wanted out of the entire situation because of the conversation they'd had a few minutes before they got here. The thought of Stin and her sleeping together again had crossed her mind more than a thousand times already.

The scary part was her wanting to do it again, …and again.

Sure, she could sleep with him again, and it would probably be the best sex she ever had since the first time they slept together—but she wanted more than a couple of one-night stands. She wasn't the type of person who went around sleeping with men, she wanted more. She wanted to be with someone who saw her as more than just a one-night stand. She wanted to be with someone who would fall so deeply in love with her, there wouldn't be a possibility of him cheating on her with any other women.

Which is why you hate him so much, right?

"Yes," she answered.

"Yes what?" Su-Lee waited on Tonia's response. "Are you saying yes to another girl's night in?"

"I wish. I need to focus on this trial like you need to focus on gathering information on that Hammerhead who can possibly destroy us all."

Su-Lee nodded. The conversation was over when Ford issued Su-Lee to go back to her favorite destination…her computer…to find out more information about the unnamed hammerhead. Tonia just wanted to head back to the cabin and work on presenting her case for the first day of the trial tomorrow morning. She'd hoped to avoid Stin for the rest of the day, but she had a strange feeling that wasn't going to happen.

Oh well, the least she could do was prepare to defend her client the best way she could in the fastest time frame possible. Maybe during that time, she would mend fences with Lex so once the trial was over, there would be nothing to worry about, and maybe Stin and Lex could finally re-establish the relationship they once had before everything went to hell with the Hammerheads. As Tonia walked along the shores of the island, she couldn't help but notice the cabins scattered all over the island. It was close enough to the Truson Headquarters yet far enough for the humans not to have a clue about what was really going on. As she continued to enjoy the summer breeze massaging her body, she noticed one of the cabin doors was wide open.

That's weird. Why would one of the cabins be open? The members always made sure their doors were locked, considering there were humans who still believed stealing was the fastest way to get rich instead of working hard for a living like everyone else did. It seemed strange that one of the members would casually leave their door unhinged.

Which was something else she needed to report to her boss to make sure he was aware of what was going on. She knew that World War III was about to erupt between the Hammerheads and the Truson S.E.T., but Tonia didn't want any part of it. She sighed. A part of her just wanted to walk away and go back to the cabin, but she couldn't knowing someone could be in trouble.

She inched closer and pushed the door farther, revealing someone sitting on the floor surrounded by broken glass and debris. It wasn't until she walked a few inches closer that she realized who it was.

"Stin?"

Tonia watched as he hung his head down, his hands balled into fists…water creeping out onto the floor. The water was starting to build when he lifted his head and stared at Tonia. His eyes glistened a deep aquamarine blue, something Tonia was intrigued and mortified by all at the same time. She shivered. The intensity of his eyes should have been enough for her to stay away. But it brought her closer to him, drawing her in like a viper to a mouse. She couldn't resist him.

"Stin?" She repeated. "Is everything okay?"

"They took him. They wanted to kill him just to get back at me, but they failed. They knew he was too strong…" Stin cut himself off. Tears streamed down his face, which he wiped away with the back of his hand.

Tonia bent down next to him.

"Who took Lex? Where did they take him?"

"I wouldn't be sitting here if I knew where he was," he said, anger spewing through his voice.

Tonia arched a brow.

"I know that, Stin. I just figured they would have left some sort of clue as to what they wanted in exchange." Tonia paused. She knew who the obvious suspects were, but she had to be sure. If she knew the Hammerheads were behind this, it would make Stin's innocence stronger than before. This would be the perfect opportunity to nail Blake and the rest of the Hammerhead Squad to the wall. In the midst of it, she would be able to establish her reputation as the most exceptional lawyer on the team.

Tonia watched as the water continued to flood around her while she waited for Stin's response. He finally lifted his head.

"What? Did you think of something?" Tonia asked, hoping it would provide some sort of clue as to where Lex could be.

"I know what they want." Stin got to his feet and stared down at his shoes, which were covered in water. He looked at Tonia. "Did I do all of this?"

Tonia nodded.

"So what is it they want?" She wanted to focus on what their true intentions could possibly be.

"Me," he replied. "They want me."

Tonia could tell she didn't like where this was going. She decided to ask anyway.

"And what exactly do you mean by that?"

"They want me to pay for what happened to Jojo."

"But you're innocent, Stin. You didn't kill Jojo. You even said it yourself that you are being set-up by the Hammerhead Squad at the courthouse," Tonia reminded him. She could feel the heat coming through the windows of the house. Sweat started to pool around her forehead. She wasn't sure if it was from the heat outside or her nerves kicking into overdrive.

All she knew was she didn't like what was about to take place.

"I know I'm innocent of all charges. I know I didn't kill Jojo, but I'll be damned if I let them hurt Lex."

Tonia paused. She wanted to think of a better solution than the one he proposed. She knew Lex meant more than his whole world…even more than her…but knew that this entire case would end up blowing up in her face as being the best lawyer on the Truson S.E.T.

More importantly, Stin was going to spend the rest of his life in prison for a teenage boy who just came into their world not too long ago. Tonia couldn't fault him for caring about Lex—she cared about him too. She didn't want another teenager dying on her watch. But the thought of watching Stin spend the rest of his life in prison for a crime he didn't commit caused her to stir. She should have been happy to see him suffer, considering their undying hatred for one another.

Something had changed.

The intensity in his eyes was enough for Tonia to let her guard down. She wanted to help Lex and Stin get out of this horrible situation once and for all—even if that meant letting go of her reputation as his lawyer.

"While I commend you for what you're doing, I'm afraid if you do this, I can no longer be your lawyer."

Stin lifted his head and glared at her.

"What do you mean by that?" he asked.

Tonia hesitated to say the words, but she knew she had to. Based on the conversations they'd had earlier, it was starting to be too much for her. Being attracted to Stin in addition to him confessing to a crime he wasn't responsible for had become too much.

You're starting to fall for him.

"It means I'm relieving myself from this case. As of this very moment, not only am I not your lawyer, I think it would be best if I excuse myself from the team as well." She couldn't believe what she'd just said. She imagined her life before she ended up here on the island of Truson and the horrible pain she suffered while she was in Africa. Dr. Madison had done her a favor by finding her body on the outskirts of Sierra Leone and giving her a second chance to gain what she had lost only to give it all up for what? Lust? Sexual desire?

Love?

"So, what you're telling me is that you're leaving the team altogether to get out of being my lawyer? You're literally going to hang me to dry once I confess to the Hammerhead Squad?" Before Tonia could respond, Stin continued. "I'm starting to think something else is going on here, and I don't like it."

Tonia stepped forward and crossed her arms.

"And what exactly do you think is going on?"

She and Stin barely touched noses before Stin spoke.

"I think you're working for the enemy."

CHAPTER ELEVEN

Working for the enemy? What the hell was he thinking when he muttered those words? He'd known who she was since they first started training to become the best Ormans on the Truson Super Elite Team. And yeah, maybe they both hated each other's guts… but to accuse her of betraying her own team? He even had to admit to himself it was a low blow on his part. Stin felt the sting of his comment when a spark of her power formed around her eyes.

"You honestly think I would betray the team and everything I have worked for to become one of *those* people? In case you haven't noticed, they have been harassing me too."

"You mean to tell me they haven't left you alone since the last attack?" Stin asked.

"No."

Stin's anger rose. The last thing he needed was to lose her to some bloodthirsty savages who had nothing better to do than make everyone's lives miserable, especially Lex and Tonia's.

"How?"

"They threatened me."

"What did they say?"

Tonia paused. Stin hated the long silence. He could tell she was debating whether she should tell him what happened. Anger boiled inside his veins.

"They hinted about killing me if the jury didn't find you guilty."

"In other words, they bullied you into not representing me?" Stin leaned over the table.

"Stin, the table."

Stin's eyes averted to his hands. The ice quickly formed around the table in a slow-moving trickle. The ice reminded him of everything he had lost so far and how much he'd failed when it came to protecting the two people he cared about the most. With one swoop, Stin flipped the table over, the ice cracking on the hardwood floor beneath it. Stin stared at Tonia as she backed herself into the corner.

Could this day get any worse?

"Lex means the world to me," he said. "Ever since he got here on the island, I did everything I possibly could to protect him. I tried to do what my father did for me before I got here." Silence escalated between them before he continued.

"My father always played ball with me, taught me how to behave at the dinner table. Hell, he even taught me to respect women even though I never listened." Stin shrugged. "I just wanted to teach Lex the same things I was taught and now…" He trailed off.

"If you want to leave, then I don't blame you. All I want is to find another lawyer that's one of us so I won't have to worry about my identity being revealed." He felt the lump forming in his throat and swallowed. Now was not the time for his tears. He needed to come up with a plan to keep Lex safe.

And he had to do it without Tonia.

Tonia took one step, then two before she stopped. Although it bothered him to see her leave, the torture of her not saying a word made everything much worse.

“I’m not going anywhere,” she finally said, lifting her hand to touch his face. “We’re going to find Lex, and we are going to get rid of these charges so we can find out who the real killer is.”

Stin’s brow lifted. A sense of hope flooded through him.

“You just said we.”

Tonia nodded.

“And I meant it.”

Stin got hard. *Really* hard. The fact that she was able to stick around after everything he’d done to her made him want to relive that one-night stand all over again. But now was not the time. He needed to find Lex and soon.

He knew what kind of people the Hammerhead Squad were. If he didn't act soon, he couldn't imagine what they were going to do to him. The question? Where was he going to start? He had an inkling of where they might have taken Lex, but he couldn't be sure. He needed more.

“What’s on your mind?” Tonia asked.

Stin gently scratched his face.

“Where to begin. I have an idea of where Lex might be, but I’m not sure.”

A sly grin crept up Tonia’s face. Stin remembered how much he hated that grin. Now, he wanted to hear what Tonia had in mind. Whatever it was, he knew it was going to be something beneficial to both of them.

“What exactly do you have in mind?” Stin asked. The suspense was killing him. Every second that ticked by was another second Lex could be killed or worse.

“We need to start with the person that washed up along the shores of this island.”

Stin thought about the statement. Lex was the one who found the unknown stranger washed up on the island of Truson before he was kidnapped. If he suspected anyone of kidnapping Lex, Gio would be his prime suspect.

"Let's go find him," Stin said.

***

"I can't believe you went off like that! What the hell is the matter with you today?" Blake yelled.

Tears streamed down Jessica's cheeks.

"I'm sorry, Blake. I couldn't help it. I wanted him to pay for what he did to my Jojo. It's not fair he's getting away with killing our daughter!" Jessica's smashed her fists against the wall.

Anger boiled inside his skin. Why couldn't she keep her emotions in check while he took care of his plan?

"Do you not realize what you have just done? You almost ruined our chances of destroying the Truson team for good." Blake took a couple of deep breaths before he responded. He carefully pointed his finger at her. "You need to control your emotions, or else you are going to be the one that ruins everything. Do you understand?"

Jessica shook her head.

"No. I want them to pay for what they did to Jojo. I'm tired of waiting. It's not fair that they get to walk around scot-free while my poor baby's lifeless body is somewhere in another animal's stomach because of that bastard!"

Blake grabbed her by the shoulders.

"Dammit Jessica, didn't I tell you I have everything under control? You need to start trusting me," Blake commanded. Blake heard a man clear his throat behind him as Jessica made eye contact with him. Blake focused his attention on the mysterious man and eventually realized it was one of the bodyguards.

"The plan has succeeded boss. We have Lex in custody."

"How is he holding up?" Blake asked, knowing what the answer was.

The bodyguard cradled his hand over his chin.

"He's been fighting everyone since we captured him, but we managed to use Poseidon to put him in his place."

Blake's heart skipped. He'd told the guards to use excessive force but using one of the deadliest poisons he'd ever known to kill both humans and Ormans with a single dose hadn't been the plan. With the anger raging inside him, Blake grabbed the bodyguard by his collar.

"What the hell is the matter with you? Lex is my only revenge against Stin and the rest of those idiots in the Truson S.E.T. If you mess this up, I'll kill you just like I killed Gio!" Blake pushed him backwards, letting go of his collar. "Where did you put him?"

"In one of the spare rooms at Hammerhead Headquarters."

Blake pushed his way past the guards and headed back toward the building.

"Blake, wait up!" He heard his wife's footsteps crunching against the grass. If it wasn't for her emotional outburst earlier, he could have eased himself into the situation like he'd planned. Instead, it became the exact opposite, and now he felt like he had to do damage control.

"Blake, slow down! Tell me what's going on."

He couldn't. Not right now. He needed to see if the kid was still alive. He couldn't afford to lose his leverage.

It seemed like forever, but he was somewhat relieved when he found Lex lying on the bed. From a distance, it looked like he was sleeping, but he had to be sure considering how potent the poison was.

"Lex," he called out. He called his name again and again as he shook him. Lex didn't move.

"Blake, who is this kid? Is this Stin's son?" His wife's voice echoed.

"Call for help," was all Blake could muster as he stared at Lex's lifeless body on the bed.

"Blake, what's going on?"

"Dammit Jessica, call for help I said!" Jessica turned and ran down the hall while Blake cradled him.

"You have to wake up. You're my only hope at making sure my plan goes as smoothly as possible. Wake up!" Blake shook Lex as hard as he could before slapping him across the face. Nothing. No response—not even a blink. He wanted to kill that bodyguard for putting him through this.

Blake kept trying until he heard footsteps barreling into the room. A short, bald man hurried to the bed and asked Blake to stand back.

"What happened to him?" the man asked while checking Lex's heart.

"One of the bodyguards gave him a deadly poison, and I think it messed up his entire system. I don't know if he's dead or—"

"What kind of poison?"

"Poseidon," Blake answered.

The doctor paused and stared at Blake. There was no time for judgment. If he was supposed to be the greatest doctor in the world, then he should have been helping Lex breathe again.

"I'm going to need the antidote ASAP."

"What kind?" Despite the Hammerheads using the poison several times to destroy their enemies, an antidote never came to his mind. As far as he knew, whatever happened and there was nothing anyone could do about it.

"I—I don't know what you mean. I don't even know what's going on!" Blake heard his wife say as the doctor grilled her about the antidote. Blake buried his face in his hands. This wasn't part of the plan. He didn't want Lex to die; he just needed him as leverage for Stin to admit what happened to Jojo.

He had too much at stake. If anyone found out the truth about what happened, he would lose everything. Blake couldn't help but stare at Lex's lifeless body as the doctor grabbed a needle out of his bag and grabbed a small bottle of liquid.

"What's that? Is he breathing? Is that what's going to bring him back?"

The doctor lifted the bottle to the light.

"Blake, you need to tell me what's going on." Jessica pointed at Lex. "Is that Stin's son? Where did he come from?"

Blake closed his eyes. He smashed his fingers on the bridge of his nose.

"Jessica, I don't have time to explain this to you."

"What is that supposed to mean? I'm your wife, Blake. You need to talk to me. We're supposed to be in this together."

Blake turned his attention toward Lex. Coughing escaped his mouth, and the color was coming back into his face. Blake exhaled.

"You were lucky," the doctor said, interrupting the argument. Despite the pigmentation of Lex's skin, Blake was still relieved to see him open his eyes. A new sense of relief flooded through him.

All he needed was Stin.

***

Ice flooded through his veins as Stin watched the mysterious man open his eyes. He had a moment where he knew he needed to transform into his alter ego and let him eat and play with the other orcas for awhile. But there was no way he would be able to get any rest or transform until he knew Lex was safe and sound at the cabin. Stin gave everyone one last look, with Ford staring straight at the man who might possibly have arranged for Lex's kidnapping to satisfy the Hammerhead's needs.

"Hello Giovanni, nice to see you again…or not," Stin said. Giovanni took a couple of swallows before he managed to speak.

"What…happened to me?"

"Your body was found washed up along the shores of Truson. You're lucky to be alive. Do you remember how you got here?"

"I only…remember being hit," he replied. His voice was raspy. He talked so low, Stin struggled to hear what he said.

"How did you get here?"

Gio shrugged.

"Don't remember."

Don't remember? His excuse wasn't good enough. Stin had no doubt in his mind that Blake was responsible for Lex's kidnapping. He wanted answers, and the only way he was going to get them was to show Gio what he was capable of. Stin grabbed Gio's shirt and brought him close to his face…so close their noses were almost touching.

"Stin!" Tonia shouted. Stin ignored her.

"Tell me what you know. Where is he? Where did Blake take him?" Stin saw Ford and Tonia walking toward him. He held his finger up, stopping them where they stood.

"I will be able to tell you everything you need to know under one condition."

Condition? When it came to Lex's life, there were no conditions. Stin shifted his weight but didn't take his hands off of him.

"I'm not going to ask you again, *Gio.* Where is Lex?"

Gio shrugged his shoulders.

"Who is Lex?"

Stin made eye contact with Tonia and Ford.

"I don't think he is aware of the kidnapping Stin," Tonia said.

"Tonia's right. He was probably in the ocean fighting for his life when Lex was kidnapped."

Stin stared at Gio and the slashes embedded in his chest. Bite marks escalated down his arms and legs. Scars revealed that whatever happened before his body floated to the island of Truson, someone or something took a huge bite out of his face.

There was no way he could be just a human washed up along the shores of the island.

"We're going to find him Stin. But I don't think Gio knows what we are talking about." Tonia laid her hand on his shoulder. "Let him go Stin, please."

Stin stared at Tonia's face before he focused his attention on Gio.

"Who got kidnapped? Who's Lex?" Gio repeated.

Stin let go of his shirt and started pacing the room. He needed to burn off this extra energy, but he knew he couldn't leave. He needed answers and right now, Gio was his only hope at achieving this mission.

"Hi Gio, I know you're probably confused about what's going on, but we need your help with a critical matter." Tonia paused.

"A sixteen-year-old boy has been kidnapped, and we are trying our best to locate him."

"I'm sorry to hear that—"

"Forget the apologies. Tell me what you know," Stin interrupted. Gio closed his eyes and shifted his weight on the bed.

"I think I know what might have happened to Lex." Gio turned his head in Stin's direction. "I know who's trying to set you up."

"What do you mean?" Ford piped in.

"Stin's innocent when it comes to Jojo's death."

"If Stin is innocent, who killed Jojo?" Tonia's question was the same question Stin had in mind as he continued to listen to what Gio had to say.

"I have a pretty good idea who might have taken Lex."

Stin inched closer.

"If you know who's behind it, then spill. Who has Lex?" Gio cleared his throat.

"There were a lot of betrayals and backstabbing when it came to Blake and the Hammerhead crew, including what Blake did to Jojo."

Tingles formed throughout Stin's body as he looked on. Whatever Gio was about to reveal had to be something to work in Stin's favor when it came to this entire situation.

"And what exactly did he do?" Ford asked.

"Blake had sex with Jojo."

Stin exhaled while Tonia gasped.

"You mean to tell me that Blake molested his own daughter?" Tonia asked.

"Yes. It had been going on for years…ever since Jojo was eleven years old. But it all changed—" Gio started coughing.

"I'll go get water." Ford managed to move to the other side of the room while Stin and Tonia waited for him to confirm their worst fears.

"—When Blake got Jojo pregnant." Stin watched as Ford gave him a cup of water. Gio managed to sit up on the bed and take a couple of sips before sending it back to Ford.

Stin replayed the information over in his head. He stared at Tonia, hoping it would deter him from thinking the worst about Blake. Stin could tell she was just as shocked and disgusted as he was.

"Blake was horrified about what happened. He didn't want Jessica to know what was going on between them. That's when he decided to come up with a plan to kill Jojo and put the blame on someone else."

"But how did Stin get into the picture? I mean, I know about Jojo having a crush on Stin, but they never made contact right?" Tonia asked.

Stin shook his head no.

"I remember telling her I wasn't interested in dating her and that she should find someone around her age. She wasn't too happy after I told her that." He paused.

"Blake must have known about your relationship with Jojo, which made you the perfect target for his agenda," Gio responded.

Stin reflected on what Gio was telling him. A part of him wanted to believe it was the truth. A lot of it did make sense, even though he found Gio's confession about Blake molesting his own daughter disgusting. There was still one question that lingered in his mind.

"Your story seems a little far-fetched, but it's possible," Ford said, interrupting his thoughts.

"But there's still one question I need to ask. I'm confused about one thing: How did you end up here?" Stin asked.

"I can explain that too." Stin stood back as Gio sat up in his bed again. "Do you mind if I move around? My legs are becoming a little stiff."

"Fine, but until we can confirm your story, we are going to have no choice but to confine you to this room since you are a potential threat to our existence." Stin watched Ford's hands ball up into fists. He was ready to transform. It had been a while since all of them transformed. Frankly, he needed to transform himself, but right now, he needed to focus on finding Lex.

"I understand. The reason why I ended up here is because Blake and I fell out over his wife, Jessica. I wanted him to stop lying to her and to admit the truth about what happened before he sent away an innocent man. We ended up fighting, and Blake won the fight."

"Okay, so that's how you ended up here. You still haven't been clear as to how Lex got caught up in all of this? He has nothing to do with this," Tonia said.

"I'm afraid he does. I'm pretty sure Blake is behind this. He purposely put the Hammerhead Squad as jury members to sway the vote. I wouldn't be surprised if Lex was an insurance policy if the jury didn't send Stin to prison."

"Can you prove this to the judge? Are you willing to testify to what you have told us?"

Gio nodded. Stin was in shock. Everything was starting to make sense now. He'd known there was something fishy about the jury members ever since he stepped foot in the courtroom. He couldn't believe how much of a fool he was to blame Tonia for something so unspeakable. A tinge of regret filled his thoughts while he focused on Gio who had now laid down and closed his eyes.

"Okay, I think we got more than enough information for one day." Ford patted Stin on the shoulder. "It's been a long day. I think we need to go home and get some rest."

Rest? How could he possibly rest at a time like this? Lex was still out there somewhere being held hostage by someone who was known to have sex with minors. He needed to find him. He couldn't bare having Lex around Blake for one more night.

He had to find Lex and soon.

CHAPTER TWELVE

What is this terrible pain burning inside my chest? That was the thought looming inside Lex as the pain enveloped him. He smelled the air in the room: Latex gloves and alcohol burned his nostrils. He groaned. He still felt lightheaded even when he knew he was lying down. What was going on? It felt like someone had taken a brick and smashed it across the upper part of his body.

"Glad to see you're up," a familiar voice said. A surge of pain rose to his skull.

"Where am I? Where's Stin? I need—I need help."

"Stin and the rest of the team are busy at the moment. They could care less about you right now."

Lex put his hands to his head. The echoes from this man's words cascaded through his brain. He wondered if this was what it felt like when teenagers decided to get drunk at parties.

If it was, he never wanted to experience it.

"I—need to go back home—"

"I'm afraid that's not going to happen anytime soon." The man took a flashlight and lifted one of his eyelids. The light burned his irises, something he'd never experienced before. His eyes were good when he walked through the darkness even when he transformed into his "rocker" image. The fact that his eyes were that sensitive to a ray of light told him something much deeper was going on.

"Where—am—I?" he asked. "What happened to me?"

"That's not important. The most important thing is that you're alive."

"Don't—feel—good. Need—to—go—home."

"Hey." Blake tapped him on the face. "You're not going home anytime soon. You can forget about Stin or the rest of the bastards coming to save you."

Lex squinted. Anger started boiling inside him as he stared at the man before him. He had seen him before. Stin and a lot of his friends had talked about the Hammerhead's reputation. He'd even heard about the most gruesome things including killing their own kind to make them the wealthiest shapeshifters on the planct.

Some of his friends called him by his first name: Blake. As he stared at him, Lex also remembered the story that spread like wildfire at his school: The death of Jojo Hammerhead.

"I—don't understand. Why—can't I…" Lex pulled on his shirt. Sweat poured down his neck and chest. He tried to loosen his shirt, but it was no use. Each time he moved, the pain in his chest deepened.

"I'm assuming you want to know the reason why I'm not letting you leave?" Blake grabbed a chair and crossed his legs. "I'll try to give you the short version of the story. I know you're pretty tired after all you've been through. I hate to be the one that has to tell you this, but Stin did a very terrible thing. He killed Jojo by turning into a hideous Orman and ripping her skin to pieces."

Lex shook his head. The story wasn't true. He might have believed it when it came to Ford, especially after he tried to go after his father, Vernon, but after Lex found out about Vernon killing his stepmother, he started to realize Ford wasn't a bad person after all.

But Stin? Stin was different from the start.

"That's not true. Stin would never do such a thing…" He took a deep breath. "You're a liar."

"I'm afraid you're the one that's mistaken," another voice boomed. The smell of pumpkin mixed with a scent he couldn't recognize seized is nostrils. The smell became so bad, he couldn't help but cough. Lex became disgusted when the ugly woman wrapped her arms around the man and gave him a peck on the lips.

"I assure you, my husband is telling the truth. Stin is a murderer and deserves to be punished for killing Jojo," she finished.

"I don't believe you. I want out of this bed. I want Stin to come and take me home now!" He tried to twist his arms out of the restraints, but it was no use. His arms tingled. He tried to imagine his alter ego destroying Blake. He balled his fist but felt the blood rushing to his head.

"I don't know why you're struggling to get out of those chains. You won't be going anywhere. I'll be more than happy to release you off of the bed if you continue to listen to what happened between Stin and Jojo.

"Are you ever gonna explain what happened to me?" Lex asked.

"You fell ill and passed out. Now, are you ready to listen to what happened between Stin and Jojo?" Both of them went silent. Lex knew what Blake was trying to do. As much as he didn't want to hear any more of Blake's garbage, the only thing he could do was listen to the lies Blake believed about Stin.

"I guess your silence means you're willing to listen to what I have to say?"

Lex continued to be silent, giving him the option of speaking further on the subject.

"Let me start off by saying Stin took advantage of Jojo after Jojo declared she had a crush on him. Did you know any of this? Did you talk about this with any of your other friends at school?"

Lex shook his head. He didn't want to talk about any of the things his friends mentioned about Jojo. The last thing Blake needed was more ammunition against Stin.

"Anyway, Jojo should have focused on her schoolwork instead of chasing after boys. Her life would have been so much better if she stayed at home like a teenager is supposed to. Instead, she had to go out and daydream about a lowlife Orman who was way too old for her."

"Really? From what I gathered, all Jojo did was crush on the guy. Can't fault us for falling in love," Lex retorted.

Blake's eyebrows creased. Lex could see the intensity of his jawline when he clenched his teeth. Small bumps went up and down his arm.

"Since you're being such a smart ass about the whole situation, I saw Stin come to Jojo's room while she was asleep. When her mother and I went to check on her, we saw Stin and her having sex. When I confronted them, your buddy *Stin* decided to run like the coward he is."

Lex shrugged.

"What happened next?"

Blake shook his head, and Lex scoffed.

"I had to beat him unconscious. Jojo admitted she was pregnant with Stin's baby. He knew he was going to be in a lot of trouble not only from us but from the Truson squad as well. So instead of admitting he was the one who had sex with a minor, he went and killed her."

Lex processed the story in his mind. He had a feeling the story had some flaws, but he still didn't have the full account about Stin going to court, just bits and pieces.

He didn't want it to be true. He knew Stin. Stin wasn't a killer. But he couldn't help but wonder what Stin was trying to hide when it came to the trial. Could it be true that Stin and Jojo got involved somehow? If Stin was the one who truly murdered Jojo, what was the reason behind it?

"You're probably wondering why I'm telling you all of this. I promised to make a deal when I initially started this conversation." Blake rubbed his chin. "I'm still offering the opportunity to give up Stin's location in exchange for your freedom."

"I'll give you whatever you want, but you have to release me first," Lex replied. "Otherwise, I'm not telling you anything."

Blake laughed.

"What's so funny?" Heat radiated through his body. He wanted to punch Blake in the face. How dare he accuse Stin of murdering Jojo? The girl was a slut anyway…everyone in the whole school knew it. She slept with half of the football team when he arrived at the Truson School for Shapeshifters. All of the boys talked about her outrageous behavior.

Lex didn't like her. From the way things were going, he personally didn't like Blake or any of these other people either. He wanted to go home. He was tired of all the lies.

"You trying to negotiate a deal. If I didn't know any better, I'd say you sound just like your father."

Lex flexed his muscles by jerking himself up. He felt the restraints loosen as he tried to grip Blake by the throat. He was only inches from choking him until darkness crept over him like the plague.

Lex screamed when Blake opened his mouth and painfully bit into his shoulder. The feel of razor blades shattered through his skin like a thousand bullets. A shrill voice radiated throughout the room, a voice Lex didn't realize was his own until his head fell back into the pillow.

"You try that again, and I will make sure you won't survive that attack," Blake said coyly.

"Oh yeah? If you kill me, then the Truson S.E.T. will destroy you." Lex wanted to see how bad the damage had been, but he didn't have the energy to move.

"Don't you think I *want* a war with those pathetic Ormans? Don't you think I want to prove to you and the whole world what kind of monster Stin truly is?" Blake took a deep breath and ran his hand through bright red hair.

"I think I've said more than enough. I think it would be best if we both sleep off the anger, huh?" Blake asked. Lex kicked the space between him and Blake.

"I want out of here! I am tired of listening to your shitty stories. You promised to release me off of this bed. I want out of this bed!" Lex screamed.

Blake strutted to the door.

"While you're falling asleep tonight, think about what I've said."

Lex heard the door slam behind him, leaving Lex with his own thoughts in the darkness.

***

Tonia's legs ached as she carefully followed Stin out into the evening sun. After the day they'd had, she couldn't help but worry about Lex's future. The most important thing out of the entire situation was to find Lex and make sure Blake got the justice he deserved.

But for now, all she wanted was some rest and a hot bath.

As she and Stin headed back to her cabin, she couldn't help ogling the gorgeous man in front of her. The puffiness under his eyes gave way to the exhaustion he felt searching for answers on someone he had only known for a short while. After spending time with him over the last few days, she could see why Lex would be so attached to him.

She was starting to become attached herself.

Stin stopped walking. Tonia froze. She was hoping they wouldn't talk about what happened at the courthouse after the trial. Maybe she was overthinking about Stin to even notice. Tonia waited and felt her heart skip a thousand beats when his eyes met hers.

"Listen Tonia. I just want to…"

"—If you want to get into another argument, let me just say I'm not in the mood for it," Tonia replied. "It's been a long day, and all I want to do is go home and get some sleep."

"I agree. I don't want to cause a fight with you. I just wanted to thank you for all your help today. I know I haven't been on my best behavior lately, and I apologize."

"Apology accepted." There. Accepting his apology didn't mean she was going to jump into bed with him. She wasn't going to give him that kind of power over her, not again. She did that once and had to suffer the consequences, dreaming about something that was never going to be a reality.

Stin exhaled.

"Thank you, I appreciate that," he said. They both had picked up the pace and were only feet from her cabin. "And I'm going to do everything I possibly can to protect you. I'm not going to fail you like I did Lex."

"As I've said before, I don't need your protection. I'm perfectly capable of handling things on my own…"

"I'm sure you are. I'm not arguing with you when it comes to that."

"Good."

"But you're still under my protection. The Hammerheads are at a full time high, Lex has already been kidnapped, and I'll be damned if I risk losing you." Stin grabbed her and pulled her close.

Bells went off in her brain. She didn't want him standing so close. She could easily hurt him with her poison any second, something that would end the business relationship she'd tried so hard to maintain.

"As of this moment, wc arc nothing more than…friends." Friends? *Friends?* She couldn't believe how much her relationship had changed with this man. A part of her wanted to smack herself for saying the word. When she saw the slow grin creeping up on Stin's face, she wanted to smack him.

"Friends." He shrugged. "At least it's a step up from being mortal enemies."

Tonia scoffed. It felt good to at least say they weren't total enemies anymore.

"I bet," she sassed. "It's been a long day. I'm ready to crash." Tonia took out her card key and slid it into the slot. Once she managed to close the door behind her, she slammed her body onto the couch. She turned herself over only to see those blue eyes staring at her again. Tingles formed in her stomach. Why was it this man was staring at her every move? She felt her heart drumming against her chest. Her alter ego stirred within her.

"Is there anything else you would like to say to me?" she asked. He stepped closer—so close Tonia moved to the other side of the couch.

Stin raised a brow.

"I'm not going to hurt you, Tonia. I just wanted to know if there was anything you wanted in return?"

A flash of pearly whites blinded her vision.

"Are you proposing sex, Stin?" She couldn't believe he still wanted her.

"Look, Tonia, we all have needs. You have needs. I have needs. Why don't we just put those needs together and…"

"…and what, Stin? I'm fine. I don't need to have sex with you. Been there, done that."

"And we can do it all over again." She opened her mouth to say something, but he instantly put his finger to her lips. "I think it's time you and I stop denying the feelings we have for one another. I know you've been dreaming about me, Tonia."

Heat flushed her cheeks.

"I haven't been thinking about you at all. My focus has been on this trial and trying to prove you're innocence. Once that's over, we are going to go back to our regular lives of frenemies." Tonia stared down at Stin's hands as he unbuttoned his shirt.

"Wha—what are you doing?"

"What I should have done after our first night together," he said. His eyes were sultry. Sexy. Tonia could easily see how she ended up sleeping with him.

Before she could protest, his lips met hers. Adrenaline ran through her as a mix of ice and poison came together in a fusion of lust and desire. Tonia's hands landed on his bare chest, trying to pry herself away from Stin but eventually surrendered once Stin massaged her tongue, causing her mouth to open wider.

Tonia moaned as Stin positioned himself between her legs, prying them open. The hard pull of his erection grinding in-between her legs caused her to pull him closer.

Her head felt dizzy with passion. Shivers went down her spine as Stin's lips made traces down her neck and chest. As he trailed down her chest, he removed one button after another, revealing her black lace bra underneath.

Stin's scent of maplewood flooded her nostrils as she felt his fingers caress the lace of her bra.

"I can't stop thinking about you, Tonia. I haven't stopped thinking about you since the first night we slept together."

"Just shut up and keep kissing me," Tonia barked. The last thing she wanted to think about was changing her mind on the situation at hand. She didn't need to feel guilty about what she was feeling *now.* She couldn't remember much of anything else. Before she knew it, both of them were naked.

Her breath caught in her throat. The lights in addition to Stin's sexy hot body made her head spin as Stin planted a final kiss on her lips and spread her legs even farther. Sparks of ice flashed through his eyes as he rammed himself into her. Tonia cried out as Stin dived deeper inside her, the world spinning with the lust and desire swirling around them.

Stin thrust himself inside her. Her slick folds were moist between her thighs.

"Stin!" He kept going, each movement sending her closer and closer to her climax.

"You're so beautiful," he murmured in her ear. Another thrust. Tonia remembered their last night together, she recalled how great the sex was and now? Now here she was, doing the one thing she swore she would never do—replay the whole night again in Stin's arms.

I have to admit, being in his arms does feel good...

Another thrust.

Tonia's thoughts faded away. The tingles grew stronger. Her heart raced. Her mouth gaped. Stin gave out one final thrust.

"Stin!" she cried for the final time. Liquid formed around his shaft before Stin collapsed on top of her, exhausted. Neither said another word as they shut their eyes and slept.

***

Sunlight crept through the windows, causing Tonia to open her eyes to its yellow rays burning her face. She shifted her weight by rolling over to the other side of the bed, away from the sun only to find herself alone. Tonia sighed. Last night still seemed like a dream, like what she had experienced faded in the darkness as soon as she closed her eyes.

Tonia grunted. The last thing she needed was another reminder of how she'd truly been feeling lately. She'd tried to pursue other men shortly after her embarrassing confession to Ford, but she felt like she was never going to move on. She remembered how she'd felt when her dreams were visions of her and Ford—a future filled with marriage and children.

Now everything had changed.

She pulled back the covers and got up from the bed. There was no use in trying to reminisce about something she knew wasn't going to be possible. Besides, it was the second day of the trial and she needed to focus on winning her case. With all the evidence piling up against Blake Hammerhead, Tonia felt confident she was going to dismiss the case against Stin very soon, which meant half of her job was finished.

The other half was finding Lex and bringing him home safe and sound. Even though Tonia had a rocky past with Lex, losing Lex to someone as sick and delusional as the leader of the Hammerhead Squad didn't sit well with her at all. The man was a sick and disgusting pig, and if he was willing to rape his own daughter, there was no telling what this man might possibly do. Tonia got up from her bed and went to her desk. She stared at the time. Two more hours before the trial began.

She grabbed a pen and started jotting down notes until she heard a knock at the door. *Who could be coming at this hour?*

"Tonia? It's Su-Lee, open up." Su-Lee? At this hour? Tonia shrugged and opened the door.

"What's up bestie?" Su-Lee said, quickly strutting inside her cabin.

"Su-Lee, what are you doing here?"

Su-Lee flopped down on the couch and shrugged.

"I'm here to give you moral support. You're going to need it after you call all of your witnesses to the stand today."

Tonia opened her mouth to respond but was taken aback by Su-Lee's expression.

"What? Su-Lee, what's wrong?"

"I didn't mean to interrupt the conversation. I was just wondering where your clean towels were."

Tonia closed her eyes. At least she knew that last night wasn't a part of her imagination after all.

CHAPTER THIRTEEN

Stin started to whistle in the shower as he scrubbed off the remaining scent of what happened last night. He smiled. After a few intense hours of sexual desire he held for Tonia, finally releasing it and relaxing into her arms had been a relief. So this was what he was missing. No wonder he couldn't establish an emotional connection with the other women after he sweet-talked them into his cabin.

He scrubbed his face. The stubs on his face were trying to grow back. He needed to keep his face nice and smooth for their next round, there was no way he should look like a bear to feel attractive. Besides, it was a great turn off for women in his opinion.

As he twisted the knob to turn the water off, memories of what happened last night flooded his brain. His chest tightened. It had been twenty-four hours since Lex had been kidnapped and yet here he was spending his time with Tonia. Although he didn't regret having the most incredible night of his life, he still felt guilty about not being able to search for Lex. The fact that Lex and Blake were in the same room made him want to kill him.

He needed to find him before Blake decided to make Lex his next victim.

But first, you need to address the issue with Tonia...

He grunted. He knew he'd said too much last night when he told her how he felt, but at least Stin admitted to what he had been feeling since the first night they slept together. He scoffed. Stin couldn't believe that the one person he'd despised all of this time was the one person he needed to fulfill all of his needs. The problem was, he didn't know if Tonia felt the same.

That was the scariest part of all.

Stin reached for the towel but realized there weren't any fresh towels available and cursed. The thought of coming out of the bathroom naked wasn't exactly how he wanted to start the day. He shrugged. It gave him another excuse to see her beautiful face. Maybe if she saw him naked, it would jog her memory of what happened last night, and maybe she'd confess to her true feelings as well.

Stin opened up the door and headed toward the living room. He tried to stop before entering once he heard another female voice in the room, but by the look on Su-Lee's face, he could tell it was too late.

"Stin!"

He shrugged.

"There's no use in trying to hide it now. I saw everything," Su-Lee piped in. She focused her attention on Tonia. "I would love to ask you what happened last night but the trial starts soon, and I don't want you to be late."

"Funny, I wanted to ask you the same thing," Ford announced. "Stin naked with one of his worst enemies on the team? Yeah, I can't wait to hear this one."

Stin threw his hands up.

"What is this? Attack Stin day? All I wanted was a bath towel to dry my ass and the whole crew comes over like it's a damn barbecue or something." Stin saw Tonia scurry past him and grab a towel from out of the drawers and tossed it to him.

"Next time maybe you should say something while you're in the shower, moron."

"Besides, what are you two doing here anyway? Don't you have people to rescue or something?" Stin said, grabbing the towel and tying it around his waist.

Ford put his hands in his pockets.

"Actually, we were here to check up on you two to make sure everything's okay. I know that last night was a little tough on both of you." He paused. "It's been rough on me too."

Su-Lee cleared her throat.

"Boss, maybe we shouldn't disturb them right now. Besides, we have to get ready for the trial."

The trial. Stin swallowed. His mind returned to Lex. He felt like an idiot. How could he possibly think about joking with Tonia and the rest of the crew at a time like this? He needed to get dressed and focus on bringing Lex home.

A part of him still needed to settle the situation between him and Tonia. Even though he expressed his feelings to Tonia, he would have been a fool not to notice she didn't say anything to acknowledge his worst fears: For her not to feel the same in return, that would affect him.

"Look guys, I really need to get ready for the trial. I'll see you when I get there," Tonia said.

"I agree. Let's go, Ford. Mandy's waiting on you." Su-Lee patted his chest before making her way outside.

"See ya' at the trial," Ford announced. He closed the door behind him.

Stin straightened the towel.

"Thanks for the towel." He wanted to say so much more, to *do* so much more to her, but he couldn't think about that right now. He had to focus on getting Lex back and away from danger. For him to do that, he needed to come up with a plan.

"What the hell were you thinking coming out here naked? Are you insane?" Tonia hit him on the shoulder, breaking his thoughts. "I thought you had—" She cut herself off.

Stin raised a brow.

"You thought I had what, Tonia?" He inched closer. He desperately needed her all over again. Sleeping with her had been the best thing that ever happened to him. But he needed more.

Stin watched Tonia as she searched the room.

"What time is it? I don't want to be late for the trial." Tonia strutted past him and grabbed her legal pad. "I didn't write down what I had to say this morning, but I'll be sure to remember it."

"Tonia, don't change the subject. I hate it," Stin objected and gently pulled on her arm. "Finish the sentence. Tell me what's on your mind."

She paused and took a step back.

"Stin, now is not the time to talk about this. We have to get ready for the trial, and we have to search for Lex."

Stin felt her slip away as she rushed toward the bathroom. Before she went inside, she stopped. Stin held his breath as she turned to face him.

"For a second, I thought it was all a dream. I—I thought you weren't really here and I felt…"

"…Angry?" Stin said, cutting her off.

"Sad," she finished.

Stin extended his arm.

"And now?" Stin watched Tonia's ruby red fingernails drum against the wall.

"I'm happy it wasn't a dream and that you're here."

Silence fell between them as they stared at each other. Tingles ran down his abdomen. As she disappeared into the bathroom, he exhaled and tried to figure out what she truly meant.

She's happy you were here. Isn't that enough?

It had to be enough for now. Like Tonia said, he had more important things to worry about. Lex was out there with Blake and the rest of the Hammerheads. He'd already failed when it came to protecting Lex. He'd be damned if Tonia got kidnapped or worse because of a conversation that could have been easily put on the back burner. She was right. Too much had happened. He needed to focus on the main goal.

He needed to find Lex and fast…

***

It was hard to control his emotions as he watched Blake sitting on the opposite side of the room. He felt the ice tantalizing his wrist, ready to give Blake the same fatal blow he gave his brother-in-law when he tried to attack Tonia. The mere thought of Blake being a frozen statue in the middle of the courtroom made him smile. As he shifted in his seat, Tonia's voice echoed into his mind, driving his fantasies of killing Blake once and for all.

"Your honor, I am here today to make a final request: I want all of the charges against my client dropped immediately." A chair echoed across the room as Blake's lawyer stood up.

"Your honor, this is absurd. Clearly, Ms. Ojai is making a mockery of what is truly the real issue here."

"Your honor, I have solid evidence that proves my client, Stin Vanderson, is innocent of murdering Jojo Hammerhead," Tonia announced. Gasps and whispers escalated in the courtroom. The judge slammed his gavel.

"Hush. I will have order in this courtroom."

Stin focused on Blake's lawyer.

"This is absolutely ridiculous. Ms. Ojai is stalling your honor. She does not want to see justice for my client—"

"—Justice for your client? I don't understand what you mean by that accusation when it is clear your client—Blake Hammerhead—is responsible for his own daughter's death."

"You little bitch, how dare you say something so filthy?" Jessica screamed. Stin watched Jessica climb over the bench to attack Tonia, but Blake protectively stopped her by holding her waist. Tonia and Blake's lawyer began arguing until the judge banged his gavel once again, this time louder than the first.

"Quiet down, everyone! Ms. Ojai and Mr. Valentino, approach the bench—now!"

Stin couldn't help but smile as Tonia and Mr. Valentino approached the bench. This wasn't how Stin expected it to turn out, but he would have been a fool to admit he wasn't enjoying the chaos.

"I would like to approach the bench too!" Blake barked. He turned to his wife, who was all too eager to sink her fingernails into Tonia's neck. After a few more minutes, Stin watched Blake approach the bench.

"Mr. Hammerhead, need I remind you that you are in contempt of court if you don't have a seat."

Stin clenched his teeth. The pain of his jawline intensified as he tried to get closer to Tonia. *No one is going to hurt her.* Anger burned inside his chest. He felt something drip down onto the floor and realized it was his own power gaining energy.

"I have a right to defend myself."

"Mr. Hammerhead, sit down. Mr. Valentino, you need to control your client or else I am kicking you both out and the case will be dismissed." The judge focused his attention on Tonia.

"What do you think you're doing in my courtroom young lady? Do you realize what you have done here?"

"Yes, I do, but this is very serious. I have evidence proving that Blake Hammerhead killed his daughter," Tonia said.

The judge cocked his head.

"Really? Are you sure this evidence is reliable?"

"Yes, it is your honor," Tonia said, confident about her statement.

"Don't listen to her. She's a liar. She's just trying to protect her boyfriend!" Blake shouted.

"I've heard enough! Got back to your table, Ms. Ojai."

Tonia walked back to the table and waited. Stin pulled down on her arm to get her attention, causing Tonia to lean down.

"What happens now?" Stin whispered.

"I must say I am not happy at what has transpired in this courtroom today. Ms. Ojai, if you have this evidence proving that Stin Vanderson is innocent, then I will allow you to present it to me this instant."

Tonia and Stin stared at each other.

"But your honor…"

"Be quiet, Mr. Valentino," the judge barked. He stared at Tonia. "What evidence can you provide for this court proving that your client is innocent of these charges?"

"I have a witness stating that Blake Hammerhead is responsible for his daughter's death."

"That's a lie!" Blake shouted. His eyes met Tonia's. "You're a liar."

"Blake, be quiet. You're going to end up in jail—" Mr. Valentino leaned his head forward before he addressed the court. "My client apologizes for the outbursts, your honor."

"There are not going to be anymore apologizes if your client cannot learn how to control himself!" The judge focused his attention on Stin and Tonia. "Where is your witness?"

"I'm afraid he's not here today your honor."

Stin cursed. He had the opportunity to end this now, so he could kill the one person that tried to harm the two people who mattered to him above everyone else: Lex and Tonia.

"Ms. Ojai, I'm not happy about this situation, but since you are determined to announce this new evidence against Mr. Hammerhead, I am giving you twenty-four hours to bring this new witness here—in this courtroom—tomorrow morning at 9:00 A.M. If your witness is not here by that time, I will move this trial to completion and let the jury decide a verdict. Do you understand?"

"But your honor…"

"Mr. Valentino!" the judge shouted.

"Yes, I understand your honor. I'll bring you the witness tomorrow morning," Tonia announced.

Stin averted his attention to Blake. He could see him and his attorney whispering about the recent events.

"Ladies and gentlemen, this trial is dismissed for today. We will resume here in this courtroom tomorrow." The judge banged the gavel for the final time before disappearing into his chambers.

"So, what now?" Stin asked.

"We have already convinced Giovanni to testify in your favor tomorrow. If he doesn't show up, we're in trouble."

***

Blake's heart drummed in his chest. A new witness? It had to be a joke. Who else could know what happened to Jojo besides Gio? His thoughts spun as he started to question who to trust when it came to his team. Was it possible Gio had told someone else what happened before he died? Blake cursed. Who else could have known about what happened?

"Blake?"

Blake squinted.

"You were supposed to do your job. How could you let this happen?"

"Blake, what's going on? Who is this surprise witness?" Jessica asked.

"I don't know. I wish I could tell you, Jessica, but I don't even know myself."

"Are you sure?" Mr. Valentino asked, raising his brow. "If there is anything you haven't mentioned before now, you need to tell me."

Blake thought about what the lawyer said.

"It should no longer be an issue, but there might be a slight possibility someone is trying to frame me," Blake confessed.

"Who?" Mr. Valentino packed up his suitcase and headed toward the double doors of the courtroom. Blake and Jessica followed suit.

"Giovanni, my personal bodyguard."

His lawyer shrugged.

"Okay, start talking. I need to know everything. I don't want any more surprises when it comes to this trial. Once was enough, you need to start talking Blake."

"I would like to know what you're hiding as well," Jessica announced.

"I don't think you've noticed, I was really trying my best to avoid this conversation until after the trial but since Tonia decided to tell lies about what happened—"

"Blake, get to the point. What happened with Gio? Is he okay?" A pang of jealousy hit him as his mind reflected back to Gio's confession about lusting after his wife. A part of him was grateful he was dead, never to be seen on this earth again.

"Gio died a few days ago. He got attacked by a school of sharks whilc hc shifted looking for food."

Blake heard Jessica gasp.

"So, what does him being dead have to do with the surprise witness they claim to have?" Blake's lawyer asked.

"He had a grudge against me. He always wanted to become leader of the Hammerhead Squad and might have told some of the other members some false information."

"Like what?"

"I don't know," Blake lied. Blake watched Jessica pull out her cell. "What are you doing?"

"I'm calling the headquarters right now," Jessica said. As his wife moved to another location to make calls, Blake focused his attention on Stin and Tonia. His heart pumped into his chest. He thought about Lex. Could he know something about the kidnapping? His mind raced about which of the Hammerhead Squad could have betrayed him.

"Where is Lex?" Stin asked. He stopped when they were inches apart.

"Excuse me, you may not talk to my client—"

"I don't know what you're talking about *Stin.*"

"Stin, don't do this. We're almost there—"

"I'm offering a deal. I'll confess to murdering Jojo if you give Lex back to me right now," Stin said, cutting Tonia off.

"I don't know where you are getting your information from, but this is totally out of line," Blake's lawyer argued.

Blake nodded. He was finally getting his wish, and he didn't have to sacrifice a young boy's life to do it. He was finally going to get away with murdering Jojo while destroying the Truson S.E.T. at the same time.

"Deal," Blake agreed. His mind fantasized about his greatest wish. He had the possibility of destroying the Truson S.E.T. for good and keeping his secret all at the same time. What better deal could he get? On top of everything else, he would be able to take advantage of being the most powerful leader on the planet.

"I'll call you later to discuss the arrangements," Stin said and walked past him, the wind tickling his cheek. He didn't even have time to blink before Blake was grabbed by his lawyer.

"What the hell do you think you're doing? Why would you agree to do such a thing?" Mr. Valentino rummaged his fingers through his hair.

Blake's attention focused on Jessica as her heels echoed through the hall.

"You know what? I think it's time that we part ways. I really appreciate your time and effort, but I don't need your services anymore."

"Blake, what the hell are you doing?"

Blake raised a hand up to his wife, cutting her off.

"Excuse me?"

"I think you heard what I said, and I frankly don't like repeating myself when it comes to these situations." Blake watched his lawyer nod his head.

"Pardon my husband, Mr. Valentino; apparently, he doesn't understand what's going on."

"I don't need you to correct me Jessica, I know what I'm doing."

Mr. Valentino held his hands up in defeat. "I don't know what the hell is going on, but I'm officially done with this case." His lawyer adjusted his suit and tie and saluted both of them. "It's been nice knowing both of you."

As Blake watched Mr. Valentino walk toward the entranceway of the courtroom, Jessica shoved him.

"What the hell do you think you're doing? Mr. Valentino was going to win the case for us. How could you do such a thing?"

"We finally got what we wanted, don't you get it? Stin's admitting to killing Jojo in exchange for Lex's life. I can let Lex go. It's all over Jessica," Blake said. Blake kissed his wife on the lips. "This is going to be the greatest day of my life." He grabbed his wife by the hand. "Let's celebrate."

***

All of the hard work she had put in when it came to setting Stin free had almost worked. They were only one step away to finally ending this once and for all. Blake was going to be prosecuted for kidnapping Lex in addition to being charged with incest and murder. She was going to be relieved of everything that had happened within the last few days, including her feelings for Stin.

Until now.

"I can't believe you are doing this. We were only one day away from releasing you from a murder charge and you blew it right out of the water by making a deal with him. Why? Why would you do something so stupid that could potentially destroy both of us in the long run—"

"—Because I care about Lex. I don't want to see him get hurt, don't you understand that? While we stand here debating on whether Gio is going to show up or not, Lex could be suffering. I can't risk it. I can't risk losing Lex, period." Stin turned his back and marched out of the courtroom.

Tonia followed close behind, her heels clicking against the concrete.

"I understand you want Lex safe and sound, but we're almost there Stin. Can't you wait until things settle down?" Tonia stopped when Stin paused and turned to face her.

"If you were a parent, you wouldn't be convincing me not to go after him." Tonia wanted to speak out, but Stin continued. "I'm sorry you can't understand where I'm coming from, but time is ticking, and I have to go find Lex. Are you coming with me or not?"

"Hey, you two! Great job on the trial today!" Su-Lee said as she approached Tonia and gave her a hug.

Ford fixed his eyes on Stin and then on Tonia. "Is everything okay?" He asked.

"Everything's fine," Stin said. He turned and continued walking down the island.

"Did I miss something?" Su-Lee asked.

Tonia sighed.

"Yeah, you missed a lot."

CHAPTER FOURTEEN

"I have a funny feeling I'm not going to like where this is going. Where is Stin heading off to?" Ford asked.

"You need to stop him. He's trying to rescue Lex, and I think he's going to start with Gio," Tonia said.

"He's wasting his time. I had to send Gio back to the Hammerhead Headquarters."

"Alone?"

"Of course not. Gabriel is with him. They are trying to rescue Lex from Hammerhead Headquarters," Ford announced. "I was trying to support you and Stin at the trial. I told Gabriel I was going to meet up with him once the trial was over. I'm heading over there right now."

Tonia thought about where Stin might be headed and grabbed Ford by the shoulder.

"Ford, I think that's where Stin is headed."

His eyes bulged.

"What do you mean?"

"After the trial, Stin made a deal that he would plead guilty of Jojo's murder if Blake told him where to find Lex."

Ford and Su-Lee said, "We need to stop Stin."

"Where is the Hammerhead Headquarters?" Su-Lee asked.

"The only way for us to get there is to transform," Ford announced. "We need to do it fast before something happens to Stin and Gabriel."

"I agree," Su-Lee piped in. The fact that Stin could be out there fighting the Hammerhead Squad alone was something she didn't want to think about. Based on the information about the Hammerhead Squad, there was a small possibility they could outnumber and possibly kill them all.

And if it was true, kill Lex as well.

"Su-Lee, call Gabriel and tell him we're on our way. Tonia, try to get a hold of Stin. I don't want him to venture out there on his own without backup."

Ford and Tonia headed toward the shore while Su-Lee dialed Gabriel's number and let him know what was going on.

***

Stin trudged through the grass, thinking about where Lex could possibly be. He couldn't back out of the deal no matter how much he wanted to. Stin knew he was innocent of everything, but right now, all he could think about was the horrible deed Blake had done to his own daughter and what he could possibly do to Lex if Stin didn't get to him quickly enough.

But where was he going to start? Where could Blake have taken Lex? His mind continued to ponder the question as his feet crunched the green grass on the ground. Where would be the one place Blake could have taken him? There was no way he could ask him now, could he? He'd told Blake he would call him to discuss further details, his hidden agenda working like a charm. But if he could find Lex and provide proof that not only was Blake responsible for raping and killing Jojo but for kidnapping Lex, Blake's case would be either thrown out, or he would be declared innocent of the charges against him. It would be the ultimate revenge for him on both counts.

In addition to destroying him.

As Stin continued walking, he realized the answer to his own question. He headed toward the water, stripping off his clothes in the meantime. He knew exactly where he needed to go. Before he was able to strip out of his jeans, his phone vibrated on the back of his leg. He scrambled to find it and scoffed when he saw Tonia's name appear.

A part of him wanted to call her back and ask her to come with him to find Lex, but after what he had done in the courtroom, she was probably calling him all sorts of names, something he really didn't have time for. He hated losing his phone but knew there was always an opportunity to buy a new onc. With that thought in mind, he tossed the phone along with his pants onto the grass and headed toward the one place Stin thought Lex was being held hostage:

Hammerhead Headquarters.

As he dove headfirst into the water, he felt his body shift. He opened his mouth to scream but stopped once his head transformed from human to orca. Once the transformation was complete, Stin stuck his head above the surface and blew out the water cascading in his throat. The water soothed his entire body. He had forgotten how good it felt to finally let the water take him to another world.

His muscles were relaxed to the point where his mind started drifting to Tonia. He knew he felt differently after what he'd been through with her. Hell, he was starting to trust her more than in the past. He began to think about his hatred for her when it came to her behavior toward Lex once she found out he was a part of the Transforments. Another part of him was scared to commit to anything, including women.

Since he became a part of the Truson S.E.T. all of his relationships were one-night stands, nothing ever serious came out of them.

You were bored. Those women were boring you. Not enough excitement.

But when he had that first one-night stand with Tonia, his feelings had changed. He wanted to know more about her—where she came from, how she landed on the island of Truson, her past life—everything he didn't care too much about before.

Admit it, dude. You have feelings for her.

And so what if he did? Hell, maybe he was falling in love with her. Why would that be such a terrible thing?

Stin, can you hear me? A voice echoed, breaking his thoughts. The voice repeated itself in his thoughts, causing him to recognize who was talking to him.

Stin, I hope you can hear me. I think I have a pretty good idea of where Blake has taken Lex. We figured you would need backup, so Ford, Gabriel, Su-Lee and I are on our way to Hammerhead Headquarters now. We will meet you there.

He wanted to protest. He had more than enough power to take down a whole army. He appreciated the backup but felt like he could have done it on his own. He would have eventually made it to the Hammerhead Headquarters, roughed up a couple guys in the process, convince Blake and Jessica about the deal only to kill him with his massive superpower of ice by freezing them for all eternally, grabbing Lex and destroying the entire building by using an enormous snowstorm to damage everything around them until there was nothing left but ice.

He had it all figured out. On top of that, it accomplished two things: Not to underestimate him when it came to his abilities and not to underestimate him when it came to the people he cared about. That attitude was what had always driven him to do the impossible. Why would this be any different?

His head began pounding. He rose up to the surface to extract the extra water in his blowhole before he went down again. This time, however, he came face-to-face with a school full of Hammerheads. It didn't take him long to figure out he was starting to reach his destination.

But first…

The school started attacking him at all angles. A chunk of his skin ripped out of his left side, the pain shooting throughout his body. He wanted to scream, but no sound came out. The ice inside his body built up to where the Hammerheads bit into pure ice, their teeth shattering onto the ocean floor. Stin flipped himself over too many times to fight them off.

There's too many of them.

He knew what he had to do. He kept spinning his body around until he was able to push his entire body out of the water. He still felt the weight of the Hammerheads on his side as he dived right back onto the water again. He needed solid ground to transform into his human form.

He tried again by lifting himself up a second time, his body twisting itself once again and landing hard on the ground. The Hammerheads shook themselves into their human form with Stin close behind.

"You think you're gonna get away with attacking us, *Orman?"* one of the men asked. Stin flexed his muscles. Icicles formed out of his fingertips. Adrenaline rushed through his veins. The one thing he loved besides surfing was a good fight.

"Gentlemen!" a familiar voice yelled. "Enough." Both of the men focused their attention on the man standing behind them. "You've done your job today. Back at the headquarters now." The two men cut to Stin and then back at Blake, wondering if they should listen.

"I think Blake gave his orders, gentlemen," Stin responded. The two men slinked back to the building as Blake walked in his direction. Stin held his hand up, stopping him from coming any closer.

"I'm surprised you got here so quickly. I tried to contact you on your cell but—"

"Save it, Blake. I told you I was going to give you what you want. Where's Lex?" he asked.

Blake nodded.

"You must really care about this little dude, huh?"

Stin's jaw clenched.

"Blake, I don't have time for games. Where's Lex?"

Blake turned his back and walked toward the building.

"Follow me," he said. As much as Stin had the opportunity to strike him in the back with his icicles, he decided that going along with Blake's plan would probably be a better option for Lex's sake.

Then after that, all hell was going to break loose…

***

Gabriel took the blindfold off of Gio and stood back while Gio searched the island.

"Where am I?" he finally asked.

Gabriel patted him on the back.

"You mean to tell me you don't know where you are *chico*?"

Gio gave the island a second look. He stared out into the water and saw fins swimming around in circles. He saw the Hammerhead statue on top of the building. He turned.

"Why am I back on the island? What's going on?"

Gabriel shrugged.

"You are leverage *Hijo.* You need to tell us where Lex is, or I'll have no choice but to hand you over to Blake."

"I told you, I don't know where Lex is."

"I'm trying to help you out. I just heard from my boss Blake knows you are still alive and that you shared information about what you know with the Truson S.E.T."

Gio shook his head.

"Blake doesn't know I'm alive."

"It's true, man. Apparently, we are going to make an exchange when Ford gets here." Gabriel cracked his knuckles while Gio shifted his weight.

"Yeah? And what deal is that?" Gabriel heard footsteps before he turned and saw Ford walk beside him.

"You for Stin," Ford said, interrupting the conversation. "If Blake drops the charges against Stin and releases Lex, you and Blake will stay at Hammerhead Headquarters."

Gio's face turned bright red. He walked up to Ford.

"May I remind you that Stin would have been charged with murder if it wasn't for me coming forward?"

Ford crossed his arms.

"I appreciate your cooperation, but I have to do whatever it takes to protect my team even if that means giving you up to keep Lex and Stin safe."

Gio scoffed.

"It doesn't matter. There has to be some sort of witness protection program for Hammerheads. All I have to do is find one."

Ford shrugged.

"Good luck with that. There's no program that exists. And before you say you can just go to the police, the government will eventually know who you are and kill you on the spot."

Gio kicked the grass on the ground.

"This isn't fair, dammit! You people should be protecting me from these monsters. I helped you nail this bastard to the wall, and now you're turning me over to him for Stin?"

The rest of the team arrived and watched as Gio got down on his knees and pleaded for his life.

"Please, I know Stin is important to you, but I can't go back to the Hammerhead Squad. They won't hesitate to kill me."

Ford opened his mouth to respond but stopped short when he heard gunshots. He ducked and searched the island. He couldn't see the shooter. More shots rang out, followed by a loud scream as Ford focused on Gio.

Gio held onto his shoulder, crying out in pain. Ford crawled to Gio and examined the wound.

"It's only a flesh wound. You're going to need medical attention."

"I'm afraid he won't be able to receive the medical attention he seeks," a familiar voice said.

Gio's eyes widened as Ford turned and came face-to-face with Blake's gun.

"I have to admit I always hated the Truson S.E.T. They felt like they had to stick their noses in everything. My plans would have worked if you two hadn't gotten involved." Blake strolled toward them.

The smell of gun powder invaded Ford's nostrils.

"The Truson S.E.T. is like family to me, and I will do whatever it takes to protect them."

"Don't worry, your team and this traitor—" He pointed the gun in Gio's direction. "—won't survive too much longer." Blake put his hand on the trigger.

Ford and Gabriel moved back when Stin came out of the bushes and tackled Blake to the ground, knocking the gun out of his hand.

"Where's Lex?" Stin shouted. "What did you do to him?"

"Fuck you."

Ford watched as Stin raised his fists and struck Blake in his jaw.

"I'll go check the building," Ford said.

"I'm right behind you," Gabriel added, leaving Stin and Blake battling it out.

***

"Blake." Jessica stepped out of the building to search the island for her husband. He was supposed to meet with her to discuss what the next move was going to be now that Stin finally decided to tell the truth.

"Blake?" Where could he be at this hour? Panic started to settle, and it only intensified when she saw two men heading toward Hammerhead Headquarters. Her heart thumped inside her chest. Where was Blake? Her answer came when she saw him and Stin exchanging blows.

"No!" She wasn't going to lose her husband to a killer. That was just not possible. The wind flowed through her hair as she ran toward them. Her feet started to feel heavier with every step she took. Anger flooded through her. She felt herself transforming as she opened her mouth and grabbed Stin by the waist before tossing them both headfirst into the ocean.

Catching Stin completely off guard, Jessica bit Stin's side, which seemed to be partially damaged from an earlier attack.

Good. Maybe I can finally end this once and for all.

She continued biting Stin while Stin swung his body back and forth, trying to get away from her ferocious teeth embedding in his skin. It wasn't until her teeth turned into ice that she knew she was in trouble. Her eyes felt frozen, and her body could no longer move.

Stin escaped her grasp as Jessica remained an ice statue, her body sinking deep into the bottom of the ocean. Her dreams of getting justice for her daughter faded away into the darkness.

***

Stin had mixed emotions as Jessica's body disappeared into the unknown. Even though he had a distaste for her as a person, if what Gio said was true, then it probably wasn't her fault for getting the wrong idea about Stin. Besides saving his own skin, he couldn't help but feel a tinge of regret about how her husband lied to her about their only daughter. Stin thought about the relationship he had with Lex and wondered if there would be a time where he would have to lie to him.

His thoughts threw him off guard as another attack lunged him forward. A sharp pain rose from behind him.

You bastard! You killed my wife! More attacks came from every angle, this time stabbing and pulling at him. He had used up most of his energy on Jessica. He found it harder and harder to fight them off.

He needed backup and fast.

He felt the darkness come over him but continued to fight them off until he had no energy left. Just as he felt his body shrinking, The Hammerheads backed away from him and fell deeper like Jessica had.

Stin, you need to transform now!

He heard the message loud and clear. It was time for him to let the water out of his blowhole anyway. Using all of the energy he could muster, Stin gave himself one final twirl and pushed himself in the air, hoping to make a successful landing onto the island. Stin knew he made it when he felt his body slam hard against the ground, causing a small earthquake to rumble and eventually stop while he transformed back into his human form.

"Transform back into the man you are, you coward." Blake did just that. A small chill went through Stin while he watched Tonia stand straight and tall, ready to defend him and herself against the bastard that tried to destroy all three of them.

Blake laughed.

"And you? I wanted to kill you the moment I knew you were going to represent Stin," Blake said coyly. "Besides, you were a part of the Truson S.E.T. anyway."

Stin felt his blood boil. Tonia carefully lifted her hand, a mist of green poison swirling around it like a whirlpool, ready to give him the final deadliest assault that would ultimately end his life, but someone tackled him from behind, slamming Blake onto the gavel.

"What did you do with Jessica?" Gio screamed. "Where is she?"

Blake swung back but missed.

"You shouldn't be blaming me for Jessica's death."

Gio's eyes widened. Stin felt sorry for him.

"She's…she's dead?," Gio mouthed.

Stin saw the sadness and rage all at the same time. Tonia inched toward both of them, ready to aim, but Stin grabbed her shoulder, preventing her from going any farther. Gio grabbed Blake by the neck.

"Where's Lex?" Gio's hand was almost the same size as his neck. "You did this. You caused all of this grief just so you wouldn't end up looking like the bad guy, but it failed." Gio tossed Blake to the ground. "I can't blame the Truson S.E.T. for this, Jessica would still be alive if it wasn't for you." Gio gave him a kick to the ribcage.

"Where's Lex? Give him up now, or your ass is dead," Stin said. "No more games. It's over Blake."

"You've wasted our time long enough. Tell us where Lex is," Tonia piped in. Blake smiled.

Another round of gunfire shattered through the sky.

"It's all over. I've lost the only woman I've ever loved because of your people." Blake pointed to everyone that stood before him. "I was going to let Lex live in exchange for your death. It's over now." Blake extended his arms out.

"As of right now, your precious protégé is officially dead."

CHAPTER FIFTEEN

Butterflies hit her like a cannon. The last thing she wanted was for Lex to get hurt. The thought of Lex being dead…she would never forgive herself. Worst of all, Stin would never forgive her for letting it get to this point. The idea of Stin hating her all over again made her sick to her stomach. They were finally making progress with Stin admitting his true feelings for her—something she would admit she felt really good about.

It confirmed her worst fears about their relationship. She agreed to being a coward and not taking a moment to express her feelings in return.

Now she may never have the chance.

She focused on Stin and Blake's swinging blows until Stin hit Blake across the jaw, the physical contact causing Blake to fall backwards onto the grass. Tonia saw a big, muscular dude come back with a blow of his own. Tonia watched in horror as both men fell to the ground. Tonia heard a slight groan coming from Stin and rushed to his aid just before water shot off his hand and onto Blake's men, turning their entire bodies into ice.

Can't let him die! He's mine!

"The only one who's going to make him suffer is me!" Tonia announced as Stin lay on the ground, bleeding from the wound.

Tonia closed her eyes and spun around until she felt the poison spread out and started hitting the men with every turn, leaving nothing but skeletons. The men left decided to run, not willing to take the risk of their own lives to save their fallen leader. Once the men disappeared, Tonia searched for Stin and saw the wound had basically healed itself using his own powers.

"Let's go," he ordered.

Tonia followed right behind him as they both ran to the entranceway. She figured it would have been smooth sailing for them to have access to Lex. But once the doors were opened, her heart sank. The expression on Ford's face was enough to confirm Blake's confession. Tonia stood back. Stin walked toward him, afraid of what he might say.

"Ford, don't look at me like that." Stin pointed his finger at him. "Don't you tell me what Blake just said out there is true."

"What did he tell you?" Ford asked.

Su-Lee had approached and rolled her eyes.

"My goodness Ford, don't you have a conscience?" Su-Lee cut her eyes to both of them. "Lex isn't dead yet. But we can't find him. If we don't find him soon…" Su-Lee cut herself off.

Tonia exhaled. The fact that Lex was alive meant they still had a chance to find him before it was too late.

"Have you been able to locate him telepathically?" Tonia asked. It was usually standard practice to communicate with the team whenever they turned into orcas. But to do it while they were still human was a long shot.

"No. He's still human. We tried, but it failed," Ford said.

Stin shook his head and pushed past them.

"Where are you going Stin?"

Stin turned.

"I don't care if I have to tear this building from the inside out. I'm gonna find Lex, and I'm gonna take him out of this hellhole if it's the last thing I do."

"I'm coming with you," Tonia piped in.

Su-Lee grabbed her arm.

"Tonia…"

"Su-Lee, I really don't need the pep talk about how dangerous it is. I need to support Stin and find Lex." Tonia stared at Su-Lee, hoping she wouldn't argue about what she needed to do to set things right.

"Mind if I join along?" a voice said. The whole team stared at who thc voice belonged to. Gio emerged from the shadows with a bandage wrapped around his arm. "I just lost the woman I love because of Blake's sick ways. I'll be damned if Lex becomes another victim of Blake's lies."

"Why would you want to help us? We were about to give you up to Blake in exchange for Stin's life." Tonia nodded at Ford's suggestion. There was no way Ford would risk losing one of his own for a potential enemy. That had always been the rules when it came to the Truson S.E.T., and Gio couldn't be the exception to the rule.

"Look, I understand. I would probably do the same thing for the Hammerhead Squad. Though I am upset about Jessica's death, I know none of this would have happened if Blake had just told the truth and paid for his crime." He stepped closer. "We have to find Lex and destroy Blake. Once we do that, then you won't have any more problems from the Hammerhead Squad."

"Sounds good to me, let's go," Stin said and strutted up the stairs with Tonia close behind. Another shadow appeared before them.

Once she saw her face, Tonia knew who she was.

"Hey, Mandy. What are you doing here?"

"I'm here to help you find Lex."

Stin and Mandy exchanged hugs. Tonia couldn't help but feel a small sense of jealously. It was bad enough that Mandy took the one person she admired and crushed all of her dreams of being with Ford. Now here she was, hugging the one man who protected her from a brutal attack that could have ended her life, the one man who had desperately stated how he felt about her.

Now Mandy was going to destroy that too.

Not this time. Stin is mine, and I'm gonna make sure no one takes him away from me.

Once Stin and Mandy broke away from each other, Mandy focused her attention on Tonia.

"Hi Tonia," Mandy said. "How have you been?"

"Good. I'm just trying to find Lex so we can go home." Tonia hoped Mandy would get the message.

Mandy nodded.

"I understand. That's why I'm here."

"Any luck?" Stin asked.

Mandy shook her head, no.

"We have to find him. He has to be here." Tonia wasn't going to give up. Stin needed her to find Lex. But it wasn't just Stin who wanted to find him. Despite their history, she would never forgive herself if she found out Lex was dead before they got to him.

Now was not the time to declare your feeling for Stin. She needed to pull herself together and find Lex.

"Have you checked this side?" Tonia asked, pointing to an empty hallway with another opening attached to the far end of the wall.

"No, I was about to check."

Tonia decided that was her cue to start looking. She overheard Stin and Mandy say goodbye to each other before Stin caught up with her.

"What was that about?" Stin asked as they turned and walked down the hall.

"What was what about?" Tonia tried to focus her attention on finding Lex by opening the doors to one of the rooms.

"C'mon Tonia, don't tell me you're still upset about Ford choosing Mandy over you?"

A light sting pierced through her heart. She had to admit it stung a little, but that it wasn't enough for her to go out to a bar and drink herself to death like before. She was finally able to move on. She had focused her sights on someone new. Somconc she hadn't expected to fall in love with.

Neither did she expect to fall in love with someone that was once considered her worst enemy.

"I'm not, Ford made his decision. I'm over it." She opened the doors to the closet and quickly closed them and started searching for any entries that might lead to a secret passageway to another room. She remembered one of her close neighbors having a secret passageway back in Africa to avoid potential enemies who wanted to destroy their house.

She wouldn't have been surprised if Blake thought the same way as her neighbor.

"Do you mean it?" Stin asked, interrupting her thoughts. "You're not upset about Mandy anymore?"

Tonia's eyes met Stin's.

"No." She wanted to relive the moment from yesterday—to be in his arms and kiss him all over again but knew she couldn't. She had to find Lex. She looked at a row of stairs on the other side of the hallway.

"Tonia? Do you see anything?" Stin asked. Once he saw the set of stairs, both of them ran down to search. Tonia was the first one that spotted Lex lying on the bed, locked inside a glass box. He appeared to be sleeping. His eyes were shut and his hands were crossed on his chest.

Please don't be dead.

Tonia rushed to the box and tried to open the door but saw the bolt latched onto the door.

"Lex! Lex, wake up!" Stin shouted as he banged on the glass door. Lex didn't move. Tonia tried to pull the door open, but the latch wouldn't budge.

"It's not opening. The latch is stuck," Tonia announced.

"Move back."

Tonia knew the look Stin gave her. It involved him using his powers to set Lex free. Tonia stood back as Stin used his hand and covered the entire lock with ice. Once he threw his fist into the lock, they ran inside and checked Lex's pulse while Stin shook him, trying to wake him up.

"I have a pulse, but it's low."

"Blake must have used some type of power to try and kill him," Stin said. Stin slammed his fist onto the edge of the bed.

"I guess it was too late for you to save him."

Tonia and Stin both stood and shielded Lex by standing in front of him.

"You were supposed to be dead," Stin said.

Blake shrugged.

"It's funny how heat can eventually take away the ice that invades the body, isn't it?"

"You stole Ford's power?" Tonia asked.

"Let's just say I borrowed it, shall we?" Blake replied coyly.

"What did you do to Lex?" Tonia was surprised by the blood boiling inside her. She couldn't believe how much of a hideous monster Blake had become, not only to his own family but to Lex as well. He needed to pay the price, and she knew that out of all three of them, one was going to end up dead.

Nine times out of ten, she and Stin were going to make it out alive.

"What did I do to him? That's not the question you should be asking. The question you should be asking is if he's still alive." Before Stin could answer, Blake continued. "I poisoned him just before you arrived *Stin*. I wanted to make sure you were a man of your word."

"What kind of poison did you give him?" Tonia thought about the different types of poison she'd heard of over the years. The crazy part about it was there were poisons that actually served as an antidote for other kinds of poisons. Maybe hers was one of them.

"Answer the question Blake," Stin roared. His fists were at his sides. Something was swimming around the bottom of his eyes. Tonia stared closely and realized it was his veins pumping the snow in his blood.

"Poseidon," a voice said. Gio emerged from the shadows with a gun pointing straight at Blake.

"What the hell is that?"

"It's a poison used on our enemies during an attack. It's potent—so powerful the Hammerhead Counsel banned us from using it," Gio announced. "Too many sharks were dying when they inhaled it. The council decided to ban it ten years ago." Gio paused. "I'm surprised it's still around."

"Just like I'm surprised *you're* still alive," Blake said. Gio raised the gun at Blake.

"Is there an antidote?" Tonia piped in. There had to be something to cure him. No way was Lex going to die because of something Blake did. It wasn't fair. Frankly, she was getting tired of hearing Blake's mouth.

Blake shrugged.

"There was one, but I think the doctor that gave it to him before is dead." A sly grin crept up Blake's face. "Now, you're gonna know what it feels like to lose someone you love."

"Camal poison," Gio said, interrupting Blake. "It might be the only thing to save him."

Tonia turned to Stin. "I can save him."

"No Tonia."

Tonia paused.

"I know you care about him, and it's not fair that Lex has to suffer because of Blake." Tonia pointed her finger at Blake. "I'm gonna save him whether you like it or not."

"I want to—" Gio stopped when Blake snatched the gun out of his hands.

"You aren't going anywhere. You and the rest of these bastards are going to suffer for what you did to Jessica and Jojo." Before Blake could go any further, Gio tackled Blake to the ground. A gunshot rang in the air. Tonia took the opportunity to run to Lex's aid while Blake's body landed hard on the floor. Gio kicked him a couple of times before finally declaring his death. Tonia got down on her knees and concentrated on sending her powers through Lex as she held his hand.

"Tonia, no!"

She ignored Stin's request and felt her powers leave her body, making a gaping hole big enough for the poison to go through. Before Tonia could complete the process, Stin gently pushed her aside and stood in front of Lex's lifeless body.

"Tonia, what the hell did you do?" Stin shouted. Gio placed his hand on his shoulder.

"Freeze him." Tonia's brow lifted. Stin shoved Gio's hand away. Gio repeated the statement.

"What the hell are you trying to do, kill him?"

"I'm trying my best to save his life. Freeze the blood now or else he dies," Gio commanded.

"Do as he says." Tonia grabbed Lex's hand and put his and Stin's hand together, the water drifting into his system until it became nothing but ice. Gio went to the other side of the box.

"What are you doing now?" Tonia asked.

"Turning up the heat. The ice will be enough to freeze the poison in his system. The point is to get the poison out of his system so he'll survive." Gio stared at Stin. "You can let go."

Stin let go, a gaping hole still visible in his hand. He took a couple of steps back and stared at Gio.

"If he dies, Blake is not the only one bleeding on this floor."

"Guys, enough already. Let's just see what happens," Tonia said. Everything was riding on Lex's recovery, including her relationship with Stin. She never realized how much she cared about him until after he rescued her from one of Blake's goons when she decided to go out for a swim. Their troubled relationship had grown into something more…something she couldn't deny no matter how hard she tried. She tried to avoid her true feelings as much as possible, trying her best to not mix business with pleasure, but after everything they went through, she didn't want to go back to the way it was before.

For the longest time, she hated his guts. She thought he was just another smug, arrogant man who didn't care about anyone but himself.

Now she knew different.

Her thoughts were interrupted by a cough coming from the other side of the room. She focused her attention on Lex and watched as he opened his eyes and looked around.

"Lex? Are you all right?"

"Where am I?" he asked. "The last thing I remember is Blake sticking a needle in me."

Stin unstrapped Lex.

"How do you feel?" Tonia asked.

Stin lifted him up on the bed.

"A little cold. There's a slight pain in my chest, but otherwise, I'm okay."

"We need to get you to a hospital. There's no way you're going to stay on the island a minute longer," Stin said.

Tonia watched Lex as he shook his head.

"What's wrong, Lex?"

"I don't want to go to the hospital. I just want to go home," Lex said. He briefly focused his attention on Gio. "Who are you?" All three of them went silent before Gio decided to answer the question.

"I'm Gio. I'm one of the men who shot your captor. Are you feeling okay?"

Lex pushed himself off of the bed and took some steps toward Gio. Lex extended his hand.

"Thanks." Gio was surprised but shook the boy's hand in return.

"That's from all three of us," Stin replied. Stin repeated the same motion, but Tonia stood back and watched as Lex held onto Stin and headed toward the doors of the building, talking like they were father and son. Tonia didn't realize how much she was going to miss out on until this very moment. The trial was officially over, there was no reason for her to overstay her welcome.

Besides, Lex can't stand you. He hates your guts, and there's no way Stin will ever forgive you after what happened. If it had to be a choice, Tonia would prefer Stin and Lex have that kind of relationship Lex needed. After the horrible episode with Lex's biological father, he was lucky to have Stin in his life.

Just like she was lucky to have Stin, not once but twice. She wanted to be a part of Stin's life and become a part of that family he created for himself.

"I guess I'm going to be the new leader of the Hammerhead Squad," Gio announced, breaking Tonia out of her thoughts.

"Yeah, I guess you are." She paused. "Before I leave, I would like to ask you to do one simple favor for us."

"Sure."

"Can you testify against Blake at the trial tomorrow? I know the case will probably get thrown out, but I want you to be there so the judge can hear what happened," Tonia said. She played the scene in her mind of how it was all going to go down, but she wanted to make sure everything was okay.

"It would be my pleasure." Tonia and Gio exchanged handshakes before Tonia walked toward the doors. She saw Su-Lee, Ford, Gabriel, Stin, and Lex rejoicing over Lex's return. She felt some moisture forming around the corners of her eyes. After the group came together, Lex walked toward her.

"You saved my life, and I wanted to say that I'm sorry for the way I treated you," Lex said.

"No no, you don't have to apologize. I was wrong for what I have done." She paused. "I guess this was my way of making it up to you."

"You did a damn good job," Su-Lee piped in. She hugged Tonia. "I think you did great."

"Thanks." She didn't feel great. As a matter of fact, she felt the exact opposite. She didn't feel like a hero. The guilt she felt was still there in the pit of her stomach, memories of what happened between her and Lex flooded her brain. Su-Lee elbowed her.

"Hey, you okay?"

Tonia nodded.

"Let's head back to the island," she announced.

***

Tonia felt the dizziness once she transitioned but managed to make the trip to the island in one piece. She managed to eat some much-needed fish and lobster on the way to Truson, which made her feel a little better. During the trip, she and Su-Lee exchanged thoughts about what Su-Lee's plans would be with Gabriel over the next few days. Tonia liked that her friend was happy about moving on with her so-called "relationship" with Gabriel. But as much as she wanted to hear more about her best friend's amazing days with Gabriel, Su-Lee quickly changed the subject.

"So how are you and Stin? Are there any wedding bells in your future?" she asked.

Tonia cringed. She thought back to the last conversation she had with Stin and how he felt toward her. A part of her wanted to go back and tell him how she really felt, but since she put poison through Lex's veins without Stin's permission…His expression reminded her of the way things used to be between them. Before this journey had begun, she couldn't have cared two cents about him.

Now that it was over, she felt…different.

"No. As a matter of fact, I don't think Stin wants anything to do with me after what happened with Lex."

"But you saved his life. I don't think he's angry about you saving the one person he cares about more than anything."

Tonia agreed. There was nothing more important than Lex being safe and sound.

Tonia lifted her head back up again and blew water out of her blowhole—the island was only a couple of swims away from where she was. She signaled her body to transform and decided to make an early jump from the ocean by propelling herself forward, her body landing hard on the dry ground. Everything spun around her, but she still managed to stand up once her vision came into focus again.

Her heart skipped when Stin stood before her, a grin spreading across his face.

CHAPTER SIXTEEN

A mix of joy and relief flooded through Stin when he saw Tonia standing before him. He didn't know what he was going to do with himself now that Lex and Tonia were safe. But something was missing from the situation. He replayed the conversation with Tonia over again in his mind. The relief was quickly replaced by fear as they both locked eyes and inched closer to one another.

He didn't want to hear the words again. He didn't want to hear that Tonia didn't feel the same way anymore, that her job of proving his innocence and saving Lex was over. He had to try again, hoping to have that final opportunity to express his true feelings.

"I really need to get dressed," Tonia said, her eyes focused on the Truson building. "I have to wrap up some things for the trial."

"So, you still don't want to revisit the conversation we had before Lex's kidnapping?" Concern and dread filled his veins.

Tonia shrugged.

"What is it that you want to talk about?" A flicker of hope invaded his thoughts as he cleared his throat.

"I—I thought maybe you would have had some time to reflect on everything that's happened so far like I've done." He gently grabbed her hand. "Tonia, I'm sorry for the way I've treated you in the past. I know I've said and done a lot of horrible things and there are probably reasons why you haven't responded to what I've told you recently."

He felt the air leaving his body but managed to calm himself down before continuing.

"I know I have a reputation of being a womanizer, but I have to admit that since the first night I had sex with you, I haven't been able to think about anyone else. I didn't even know how lonely I felt until I got to know you that night."

"We were both drunk, Stin. People do crazy things when they are drunk," Tonia said.

"I agree, but that one drunk night changed me." He inched closer. "I think I've found the woman I was looking for. The other day, I was approached by someone at a bar…"

"…Where?" Tonia asked, interrupting the conversation.

Stin shook his head.

"It doesn't matter. The point is, this woman made me realize just how lucky I was to have someone special in my life. I could have slept with her, but I didn't. All I could think about was you."

"So what does that mean for us?" Tonia asked. Stin saw the twinkle in her eyes before he cradled her face with his hands.

"It means I want a relationship with you." He paused. "It means I want to spend the rest of my life with you."

Whew! He'd said it. He'd said the one thing he thought he was never going to say. Who would have thought he would have feelings for the one person he despised? It didn't matter now. This was it: This was the moment where she had to tell him how she really felt. No more running, no more dodging him or his feelings for her.

"Stin, I—I don't know what to say…" The conversation stopped short as Stin watched Tonia cradling her belly with her arms.

"Tonia? Tonia, what's wrong?" Fear flooded through him as he watched her collapse on the ground.

"I need help! Somebody help!"

***

The room spun around her when she opened her eyes the first time. She closed them again. Darkness flooded through her vision. She could hear other voices echoing in the room.

"What did you do, Stin? Don't tell me you two got into another argument," one voice said.

"Ford, it wasn't like that. One minute we were talking about how we felt about each other and the next moment, she passed out," Stin said.

A brush of air massaged her face. She opened her eyes again and searched the room, making contact with Lex as he stood up.

"This was all my fault. I shouldn't have been so angry with her when it came to the past. I thought I was trying to protect you," Lex piped in. "I thought she was going to hurt you the same way she hurt me." Lex shook his head.

"Look!" Tonia saw Su-Lee glance and point to her. "She's awake." All eyes focused on her. Su-Lee inched closer. "How are you feeling?"

"I'm fine. I don't understand why everyone is so worried about me. I'm pretty sure it's nothing but a stomach bug." Tonia saw Ford scratch his in-grown beard.

"A stomach bug wouldn't make you pass out like that. When was the last time you've eaten?"

"Or transformed minus our trip here?" Su-Lee asked. A sigh of relief flooded through her when a knock at the door interrupted the conversation. A short, dark-skinned woman stepped inside with a clipboard in her hand, the door slamming behind her. She flipped through the pages.

"So, what's going on, doc? How is the patient doing?" Su-Lee motioned a semi-circle in the air, hoping the doctor would share whatever information she had in her notes.

"Congratulations are in order," the doctor said. "You're three days pregnant."

"Pregnant?" The word echoed in her brain. Tonia shook her head. "How? Normally, you wouldn't be able to tell in three days. That's impossible."

"Not really," Ford replied. "If you look it up in the Book of Truson, there are a few stories where women's pregnancies moved very quickly due to their alter egos and hybrid nature."

"There's no mistake about it. We did a blood test to figure out what was going on. You're definitely pregnant, and it seems there is a bit of malnutrition, so I suggest you start eating more."

"Is the baby okay?" Tonia asked. Her heart pounded. She was going to be a mom! Another life was coming into the world, and she needed to be prepared whether she liked it or not.

"Well, since we're bringing another life into this team, I think we should set things right between us." Stin grabbed her hand. "I should have been better prepared when it came to this situation, but considering everything that has happened, I didn't have the opportunity to ask this question or buy you the one thing that would have sealed the deal but…"

"Hold it, Stin," Ford interrupted. "I'm afraid we might have a problem here."

Tonia's eyes darted from Ford to Stin. What the hell was going on?

"Why the interruption? I think Stin was about to say something really important," Su-Lee said.

"Not if it means breaking her heart." Ford inched closer. "I'm not going to let you use her like you did in the past. She's my friend as well as the most effective member of our team."

"Ford—"

"I'm not finished Stin. I think that whatever is going on with you two needs to end. The case is over, you proved your innocence. When it came to Dr. Madison, I think she put one of those rules in place for situations like this…"

"Boss—"

Ford raised his hands.

"No more excuses Stin. I mean it. As your boss, I'm ordering you to stay away from Tonia."

Stin stared at Tonia.

"Well my friend, that's gonna be a real problem because we're now officially parents in addition to husband and wife."

"What?" Tonia swallowed hard. She couldn't have heard what he just said. Husband and wife? She admitted that having a relationship with him didn't seem like a bad idea after everything they had been through, but to be husband and wife? She heard gasps around the room.

"Husband and wife?" Tonia repeated.

"Yes." Su-Lee clapped her hands wildly.

Ford's mouth dropped before Mandy approached him and gently whispered something in his ear, causing him to close it shut.

"I wanted it to be special, but what's more special than right now?" Stin paused. "I know I don't have a ring, but I was wondering if you would do me the honor of being my wife?"

Tonia was speechless. What else could she say? She was having his baby, and now here Stin was vowing she would be his wife for the rest of her life. She nodded.

"Yes Stin Vanderson, I will marry you."

***

One Year Later

The house Stin and Tonia agreed to buy was all decked out for the biggest wedding of the year. A massive spray of flowers adorned the staircase as Tonia prepared to walk down the aisle surrounded by her team. Her second family watched her progress as she went down the stairs wearing a short but slim wedding dress laced with white flowers across the shape of her body. Butterflies nested in her stomach when she saw Stin turn and smile. She smiled back when she saw her little bundle of joy in Stin's arms as he carried her down the aisle. Sharlene Vanderson giggled at her mom as Tonia reached her arms out.

"Are you sure you want to do this with her in your arms? I'm not going to be able to exchange rings with you if you are holding her."

"Don't worry, Su-Lee will hold her while we exchange rings," Tonia announced. "I want Sharlene to be close to me. I don't want to put her down until all of this is over." Tonia looked at Sharlene and smiled again. Life couldn't have been any more perfect than this very moment. There was no way she wanted Sharlene to miss the excitement of her parents' big day.

Tonia looked at Stin's hands as Ford recited quotes from the Book of Truson. Tonia and Stin exchanged vows. Tonia exhaled as the ceremony came to a close.

"You may now kiss your bride," Ford announced. Sharlene cooed. Stin leaned over his daughter.

"Would it be all right if I kiss your mother now?" Stin asked. A smile came upon Sharlene's face before Tonia gave Sharlene to Su-Lee to kiss her groom. A round of applause erupted in the room. Tonia watched Stin's lips as he leaned forward, his tongue pressing through her mouth. Just as the kiss was starting to heat up, it was broken to another round of cheers. Sharlene let out a huge cry but eventually settled down once it was time for their dance as a married couple. As Tonia wrapped her arms around Stin, one question came to mind.

"Stin?"

"Yes, my beautiful bride?"

"Do you think it's fate that we're here?"

Stin chuckled. "Yes. It's more than fate. It's an Orman's fate."

Live the adventure all over again!

Missed out on the first book of the popular Truson S.E.T. Series? Don't worry, you can purchase *An Orman's Revenge* at the following retailers online: Amazon, Barnes and Noble, Kobo, Baker and Taylor, Apple books, Playster, Hoopla, 24 symbols, and other online retailers nationwide! Order your copy today!

Liked the book you've read so far? Whether you loved it, hated it, or somewhere in-between, please be sure to comment on Amazon and other retailers nationwide to let me know your views on the books. Thank you!

About the Author

Dominique Gibson knew she wanted to be a writer ever since she sat down at her plastic table and started writing stories out of sheer boredom at eight-years-old. Several years later, she decided to pursue a bachelor's degree in Fiction Writing from Columbia College Chicago. After pursuing a degree in Early Childhood Administration to support her career in Early Childhood Education, Dominique decided to go back and pursue a degree she always wanted: An MFA in Creative Writing, which she is now pursuing at Southern New Hampshire University. To learn more about her work, please visit www.dominiquegibsonauthor.com Dominique Gibson on Facebook, and @dominq79453763 on Twitter.

www.ingramcontent.com/pod-product-compliance
Lightning Source LLC
Chambersburg PA
CBHW070631310726
48982CB00001B/243

* 9 7 8 1 7 3 2 9 5 7 4 5 9 *